"That man you saw in the forest is very high up in the drug trade."

"So that's why he sent his henchman after me." Sierra's voice filled with anxiety.

Joseph turned the key in the ignition and pressed the gas. He wished there was something he could say to lift the burden of worry from her. Sometimes silence was the kinder choice over saying something trite or untrue.

The car rolled up a long hill. "Kind of like a roller-coaster ride," he said, hoping to distract her from her worry. He aimed the car downhill and coasted, lifting his foot off the gas.

"Yes, I guess. Never thought of it that way." She sounded a million miles away as she stared through the windshield.

The car picked up speed. Joseph pressed the brakes, but the car rolled even faster. So that was why they'd been lured out there.

The brake line had been cut.

Ever since she found the Nancy Drew books with the pink covers in her country school library, **Sharon Dunn** has loved mystery and suspense. Most of her books take place in Montana, where she lives with three nearly grown children and a spastic border collie. She lost her beloved husband of twenty-seven years to cancer in 2014. When she isn't writing, she loves to hike surrounded by God's beauty.

Books by Sharon Dunn

Love Inspired Suspense

Dead Ringer
Night Prey
Her Guardian
Broken Trust
Zero Visibility
Montana Standoff
Top Secret Identity
Wilderness Target
Cold Case Justice
Mistaken Target
Fatal Vendetta
Big Sky Showdown
Hidden Away
In Too Deep

Texas Ranger Holidays

Thanksgiving Protector

IN TOO DEEP

SHARON DUNN

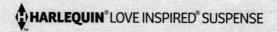HARLEQUIN® LOVE INSPIRED® SUSPENSE

Recycling programs
for this product may
not exist in your area.

LOVE INSPIRED BOOKS

ISBN-13: 978-1-335-54406-3

In Too Deep

Copyright © 2018 by Sharon Dunn

www.Harlequin.com

Printed in U.S.A.

Therefore if any man be in Christ,
he is a new creature: old things are passed away;
behold, all things are become new.
—2 Corinthians 5:17

ONE

Panic invaded Sierra Monforton's nerves as she sprinted through the brush that led to the lakeshore. Trevor Bond, a troubled fifteen-year-old boy from the youth group she headed up, had not been on the road where they'd agreed to meet.

As she stepped to the edge of the brush, a fog rolled over the lake and crept along the rocky shore. The calm of the night sky twinkling with stars stood in opposition to the fear that hounded her. Trevor's words from their phone call less than half an hour ago pounded in her brain. "Miss M, I'm here at Fishermen's Crest to get drugs to sell. I don't want to go back to using, but sometimes everything just seems so hard. Help me."

She'd talked him out of his plan and agreed to pick him up. He had ridden his bicycle out there and would not be able to get away fast enough before the drug dealers showed up. Depending on how deep Trevor was already in with these dealers, he might still be in danger once she got him back to town. But she'd deal with that when she had to. Right now, she needed to get him home safe with his younger sister, Daisy, and foster mom.

And now Trevor was nowhere to be found. A hundred violent images crashed through Sierra's brain as she scanned the beach. What if the drug dealers had shown up early and been angry about Trevor's change of heart? What if Trevor had run away out of shame and would end up back on the streets of some city?

She ran along the rocky shore, calling out Trevor's name. Silence answered back. She didn't know exactly where the drug dealers had planned to meet Trevor, but Trevor said he'd be safe on the road. Why, then, hadn't he stayed there and waited for her?

Another, more sinister thought played around the edges of her mind. Everyone in Scenic View knew about her fight to get kids clean and to push the dealers out of town. Trevor had used and sold drugs before. He was only six months clean. What if he was setting her up so the dealers could harm her?

She took in a sharp breath. She cared about that kid. She didn't want to think the worst of him. And yet she knew firsthand the world he was considering going back to. When she was only a year older than Trevor, she had been headed down the same destructive road.

The sound of footsteps caused her to glance up the shore. A man in dark clothes emerged from the fog, jogging toward her along the rocky beach.

Even at a distance, she knew the man wasn't Trevor. Trevor was a short, skinny kid. This man was muscular and tall. What were the chances of a man running on a rocky beach not being connected to the drug deal about to take place? Afraid for her own safety, she slipped back into the brush. As the man ran past, she recognized who he was. Her heart beat a little faster when she saw the gun in his waistband.

Though she'd never met him, she knew Joseph Anderson by sight. He'd taken over management of the skateboard shop only a few weeks ago. The kids in her youth group raved about him. Apparently, Joseph had charisma when it came to winning the hearts of teenagers.

Scenic View, Idaho, where she lived, was a small, close-knit community. Though the lakes attracted part-time residents who owned second homes here, the people who stayed year-round and had been here for generations were the core of the town.

Sierra slipped deeper into the brush. Joseph

ran as though on a mission. The gun was cause for alarm. It couldn't be coincidence that he was in the very same area where a drug deal was about to happen. Sierra clenched her jaw. Drug activity with teens had been on the rise recently. The skateboard shop would be a perfect front for selling drugs to kids. If Joseph Anderson was up to no good, she would see to it that he couldn't hurt the teenagers she cared so much about.

Joseph disappeared around a bend. She stepped out and ran after him, not to confront him but to see what he was up to. Maybe he would lead her to Trevor. She knew she might be risking her own safety, but right now she could think only of Trevor and the other kids. If she witnessed anything shady with Joseph, she would leave and tell the police.

Trevor had sounded so lost and filled with shame on the phone. At least the boy had taken her up on the offer she gave all the kids and called her before he did something destructive. She hoped she was right about him.

Sierra's tennis shoes padded over the rocks. She slowed as she rounded the curve. Up ahead was a structure everyone referred to as Old Boat, a thirty-five-foot recreational trawler that had been scuttled here years before. Kids came to this area to build bonfires and party.

She didn't see Joseph or Trevor anywhere.

Half in the water and half on shore, the boat listed to one side, creaking as the waves bombarded it.

Something rustled in the brush farther inland. She saw a flash of red. Trevor always wore a red coat. She darted toward where she'd seen movement. She could hear the noise of someone racing through the brush, back toward the road. Maybe Trevor had panicked standing in the dark waiting for her to pick him up. At least he was headed in the right direction.

Her feet smacked the softer ground. She stepped into a clearing, about to call out Trevor's name when she spotted a man, neither Joseph nor Trevor, kneeling over an open satchel. He held something in his hand.

He looked like a businessman about to board a plane; he was definitely not dressed for the outdoors. Moonlight washed through the trees. He turned to look at her. She saw his face as he grimaced at her.

Because the moment had become almost surreal, it took her a second to register that what he held in his hands was a brick of some kind of drug—cocaine, heroin? Moonlight reflected off the metal on the large face of the watch he wore. She cast her gaze downward and then took a step back. The entire satchel was filled with drugs.

"Well, this is bad timing!" Rage tainted his words.

Time seemed to slow down as the man stood up, pulled out a gun and aimed it at her. On instinct, she turned and sprinted back toward the road. A shot whizzed by her so close it hurt her eardrum. Her heart pounded out an intense beat as adrenaline surged through her, feeding her instinct to stay alive.

Footsteps echoed behind her and then off to the side. Another shot zinged through the air. The man had positioned himself between her and the road. She sprinted deeper into the brush. She'd have to run parallel to the road until she could put some distance between herself and the shooter in order to get back to her car and escape.

His footsteps never let up. She could hear him moving through the brush. She ran, willing her legs to pump harder, go faster.

Then a shot came at her from behind, from a different direction. She caught a glimpse of a second man, his baseball hat just visible above the brush. A new wave of fear swept over her. Two men were shooting at her. She ran haphazardly, trying to stay close to the road but knowing that escape route was no good. She couldn't shake the first shooter.

She pivoted and headed back toward the shore. Another shot sounded through the night.

A body crashed into her from the side, taking her to the ground. She lay on her stomach with the man on top of her.

Terror gripped her as she tried to wiggle free of the man.

"Could you be any noisier?" The man's voice came out in a harsh whisper. "You sound like an elephant at a dance party."

She could hear the other two men moving through the brush. One shouted a command at the other.

"Get off of me."

"I will. But you need to be quiet." He took his knee off her.

She flipped over. Joseph Anderson stared back at her and put his finger to his lips. Fear struck a new chord inside her. What was going on here?

Joseph leaned close and whispered in her ear. "Come with me. I'll get you out of here."

Her instinct was to pull away and to run. He had a gun. Was he involved with those other men? Did he intend to hurt her? Or was he a rival drug dealer and she'd been caught in some sort of turf war?

She shook her head.

The two shooters closed in on them.

Sierra rose to her feet prepared to run away from Joseph. She'd take her chances on her own. She could follow the shoreline back into town or try to get to her car. She turned and sprinted.

Joseph was right on her heels.

He grabbed her from behind, spun her around and gripped her wrist so tightly she couldn't get away. "I'm trying to keep you alive."

Her heart pounded as she tried in vain to pull away. "What are *you* doing out here?"

"I might ask you the same thing," he said.

He pulled her through the remainder of the brush down to the shore, where a motorboat waited in a cove. He lifted her up and put her in the boat. "You'll thank me later."

She doubted that. She felt anger toward anyone who pushed drugs on kids. Drugs ruined lives. Was that what Joseph was up to?

She moved to get out of the boat just as Joseph pulled the starter rope and the engine sputtered to life. The two shooters emerged through the brush. One, the man she'd seen with the drugs, looked right at her and then slipped back into the trees. The other man, the one wearing the baseball hat, lifted his gun. A red dot appeared on Sierra's chest. She ducked down in the boat.

Sierra had no choice. If she ran back on shore, she'd be shot for sure. She had to stay in Joseph's boat.

But just what did Joseph have in mind? Why had he kept her alive?

Undercover DEA agent William Joseph Anderson glanced over his shoulder as a gunshot shattered the silence on the water.

The woman he'd pulled out of the forest lay flat in the boat. What had she been doing out there, anyway? Certainly not going for a stroll on the beach. Her interference messed up his investigation. Were the two thugs after her because she'd betrayed them?

Maybe she was trying to horn in on the drug activity.

Whether she was innocent or guilty, it was clear she was under threat. Now that he'd saved her life, she might have valuable information she'd share out of gratitude and a desire to destroy the men who were after her. As long as he could get it without giving up who he really was. At all costs, he had to maintain his cover.

Earlier in the day, Joseph had heard talk in the shop that a big drug distribution was about to go down at this spot. Other agents had traced a shipment out of Mexico headed to the northwest. It wasn't hard to put two and two together.

He'd come out to this part of the shore not to interfere with the transaction, but to see if he could spot who the players were. Investigations like this took a long time. A lot of information had to be gathered, or they ran the risk of the big players slipping from their clutches.

It was nothing to arrest the low-level dealers; most were kids just trying to support their own habit. DEA was after the big fish, whoever was behind this point of distribution. At best, they had blurry photos of him. Or pictures of the back of his head. His only identifying characteristics were that he dressed well and he often wore a large-faced gold watch.

He revved the boat engine. When he glanced over his shoulder, the men on shore were still taking aim at them. He'd come in the boat because he could anchor it in a cove unnoticed and sneak up to the site where the transaction was supposed to happen. A car parked on an underutilized road would have called attention to itself.

The fog enveloped them. To lessen the risk of hitting something, he clicked the boat down to an idle. It had been at least five minutes since the last shot was fired. The woman sat back up. He heard water lapping around the boat, but could see only a few feet in any direction.

He kept his voice low. "So do you want to

tell me what you were doing out there at this time of night?"

"What were *you* doing out there?" Suspicion clouded her words.

He had to assume his cover wasn't blown. "I like going out there at night. It's quiet."

"If you must know, I went up there to pick up a kid before he got himself into trouble. Trevor Bond is in the church youth group I help out with."

So she ran a church youth group. A perfect way to build trust with kids and then get them hooked. "I know Trevor. He comes into the shop." Trevor was one of the quiet ones. It broke his heart to think of any of those kids using. "He seems like he has his act together."

"He's only six months sober. He's struggling not to go back into that life. To stay away from the people who got him involved in the first place."

He caught the note of passion in her voice.

"Anyway, I'm worried about him," she said. "I still don't know where he went or what happened to him." She lowered her voice half an octave. "Or why he ran away. Maybe he's already in too deep."

Trevor sounded a lot like Joseph's little brother, Ezra. For Joseph, being a DEA agent was personal. Always a quiet kid, Ezra had died of a drug overdose when he was just seventeen. Joseph had been a junior in college when he got the call about Ezra. Such a waste of a beautiful life. His heart still ached over the loss.

Though he was not ready to let go of all his suspicions, he thought he detected genuine concern in her voice when she talked about Trevor. "What is your name, anyway?"

"Sierra," she said. A moment of silence passed before she spoke again. "Where are you taking me?"

He glanced over at her. "I'm taking you home."

She met his gaze. Her black hair was pulled back in a ponytail, and her blue eyes were the color of robin's eggs. There was something almost cute about the way she pulled the sleeves of her hoodie down over her fingers. She really didn't act like a drug dealer. All the same, she could be a girlfriend of one of those men. The shooters certainly seemed to want to take her out. Men like that didn't put up with betrayal on any level.

It would be foolish to let go of his suspicions just yet. In any case, he was still irked about her messing up his surveillance.

"Why don't you take me to the police station? I need to report this. And unless Trevor headed back home, he's still missing."

He wasn't sure what to say to that. Because

they suspected one of the local cops was tipping the dealers off, DEA didn't want the city police getting wind of their activity.

"Or you can just take me to my car," she said after he didn't answer. "I can deal with this myself."

"Obviously it's not safe to go back there. You can go back tomorrow and get your car," Joseph said. Her thinking was a little messed up, which was a normal response to the trauma of being shot at. Really, she was handling things quite well overall.

Joseph slowed down, so he could hear above his own motor.

She turned slightly in her seat. "What is it?"

"I thought I heard another boat."

The fog hadn't lifted at all. He didn't see light anywhere.

Sierra whirled to one side and then the other. Her voice faltered. "I hear it, too."

Joseph killed the motor. He doubted anyone was out for fun on a night like this. The other boat seemed to be circling around them, the motor growing louder and then fading. The motorboat swayed in the water as waves suctioned around it.

"They're looking for us," Sierra whispered. Her words were iced over with terror.

Joseph crouched. "Stay low." Did they wait

here and hope the searcher gave up, or did they risk making noise while trying to escape?

He wondered, too, why they were even coming after Sierra and him. He and Sierra been scared off, so why hadn't the two men just gone back to their planned transaction? Why draw attention to themselves by hunting them down?

A light broke through the fog with the intensity of a knife slicing meat. Joseph could see the outline of a larger boat—and the man behind the helm lifting a gun. It was the man in the baseball hat. The one who had taken aim at them on the shore.

Joseph started the engine and pulled forward. The shot echoed around the boat and had probably lodged in the hull somewhere. His boat gained speed.

The other boat was eaten up by the fog, but not before another gunshot echoed around them. Joseph turned the throttle, hoping to put distance between himself and the other boat.

The roar of the other boat's motor remained steady in intensity.

His boat slowed and vibrated.

"What's wrong?"

He gritted his teeth. "We're in shallow water filled with reeds. We're not going to be able to get anywhere." The disorientation from the fog had caused him to get too close to the shore. He revved the throttle, hoping to make some progress.

The other boat rammed into them. Their boat shook from the impact. The man leaped off his boat and reached for Sierra. She screamed and struggled to get away. Joseph lunged toward the man who had his hands around Sierra's neck.

Sierra twisted her body in an effort to escape his grasp. Joseph heard a loud splash as Sierra and the man both fell into the water. He could see only flashes of movement in the fog.

He dove into the blackness, praying he wasn't too late to save Sierra from the clutches of the man who sought to kill her.

TWO

Sierra's lungs threatened to fill with water as darkness and cold enveloped her. Pressure let up on her neck, but the man continued to grab at her clothes, seeking to hold her down and keep her under.

She struggled to get away, bobbing to the surface, gasping for air. She caught sight of a baseball hat floating on the water's surface. The man grabbed her once more. She got a good look at him before he dragged her underwater again. She went limp, hoping that playing possum would make the man give up. He held on.

She couldn't hold her breath much longer. Her world seemed to be getting blacker and colder.

She kicked her legs in a final attempt to break free.

Another set of hands grabbed her from above and yanked her to the surface.

She gulped in air as the waves rushed around her.

Joseph's face was very close to hers. "This way."

She saw him swimming for only a few seconds before the fog engulfed him. She could hear Joseph's hands and feet slicing through the water. She followed the sound. The fog caused her to lose her sense of direction. They must be swimming toward the shore. The attacker blocked their way back to the boat. It was useless at this point, anyway.

Noise of her attacker swimming through the water behind her made her move faster.

Joseph called back to her, his voice like a lighthouse beacon. "This way!"

She lifted her hand above her head and kicked her feet, trusting that Joseph was leading her to safety. It was blind trust on her part. Why would a drug dealer be saving her? But she had no choice. She wasn't sure why, but he'd pulled her from danger twice. She had a chance of getting out of this alive if she followed Joseph.

Death was a certainty if she didn't. The other man was still moving through the water toward her.

Closer to the shore, the fog lifted enough that she could see Joseph as he stood up and walked onto the rocky beach. She put her feet down in the waist-deep water.

She was jerked back as her attacker grabbed her by the collar. He clamped his hands on her shoulders, seeking to push her under in the shallow water.

She twisted free by angling her body to one side. She ran until she was in calf-deep water. The would-be assassin grabbed the hem of her hoodie. As she struggled to get away, she heard Joseph plunging back through the water.

Joseph landed a blow across the man's face and then to the stomach. The man groaned and doubled over. Joseph clutched the sleeve of her hoodie and guided her toward the shore. The shallow water weighed on her legs as she pushed through, until her feet touched the hard surface of the beach.

She glanced over her shoulder as they bolted toward the brush. The attacker had recovered and had just stepped on the shore.

Sierra sprinted beside Joseph as the brush turned to evergreen forest. They ran for at least ten minutes. She'd grown up exploring these woods, but it was much harder to navigate in the dark.

She stopped for a moment to catch her breath. "Do you know where you're going?"

Joseph bent over, resting his hands on his knees and sucking air between each word. "Maybe you could help me. I'm new in town, remember?"

Pounding footsteps behind them told her they

needed to keep running. Sierra took the lead, zigzagging around trees, searching for a landmark that would orient her.

If she could figure out where the road was, they might be able to get back to her car and escape. As they darted through the evergreens, their pursuer stayed about ten paces behind them.

Fatigue settled into her leg muscles. She shivered from being soaking wet. Though it was summer, the nighttime temperatures only made her colder.

Joseph grabbed her and pushed her to the ground. Fear shot through her. Had he just been waiting for a chance to do her harm? They'd landed in a shallow ditch.

He signaled for her to be quiet as he pressed low to the ground.

Their pursuer ran past. So that's why he'd knocked her down.

They waited until their pursuer disappeared into the trees and his footsteps faded in the distance.

Joseph jumped to his feet. "He might double back when he figures out we lost him. Where are we going?"

She glanced around, recognizing a rock outcropping though it was covered in shadows. "I think I can get us back to the road."

She sprinted uphill, still cold, still out of breath. The ground leveled off. Now that she knew where she was, she ran faster. Joseph kept pace with her.

She took in a deep breath when her feet touched the hard-packed dirt of the country road. She'd parked on a shoulder just around the curve. Sierra sprinted as a sense of relief filled her. In less than a half hour, she'd be back at her place, sitting in dry clothes in front of the fire. She'd be safe, but she still didn't know about Trevor. She'd have to tell the police about the attack. If Trevor wasn't back at his foster home with his sister, maybe the police could find him. Maybe they would be able to figure out if he had set her up.

A question raged through her head as her feet pounded on the road. Why was that man in the baseball hat so bent on killing her? The question made her shudder. With God's help, she would get over the attack.

She rounded the curve to where her car was sitting, and slowed her pace as she drew nearer to it.

Joseph came up beside her. "Looks like they slashed your tires."

Despair spread through her like liquid poured on a napkin. She kicked one of the tires. "Guess they wanted to make sure I couldn't get out of here." The notion sent a whole new wave of fear through her. The man she'd seen earlier with the drugs must have done this to her tires while Baseball Hat chased them.

A crashing sound in the trees down below signaled that the attacker was back on their trail.

They needed to get off the road before they were spotted.

Joseph pivoted and headed back toward the shore with only a vague plan in his head. They weren't going to outrun this guy. Joseph had lost his gun somewhere in the water. They had to find a hiding place. This guy was persistent beyond anything that made sense.

They came out beside the boat that had been wrecked on the shore. It was a big boat with a belowdecks area. Lots of places to hide and take a man by surprise if needed.

With Sierra at his heels, he climbed the ladder and slipped below deck.

She followed him. "Don't you think he'll look in here?"

"We'll be able to hear him if he comes on deck. It's two against one in a confined space. We can take him by surprise. Let's see if we can find a good hiding place."

Below deck consisted of several rooms, including what must have been a galley kitchen at one time, though it looked like it had been scavenged over the years. A skeleton of a counter remained. Sections of the countertop had been pulled off. Doors were missing from the cupboards. A dirty frying pan lay on the floor.

"I don't see a place to hide." Sierra paced through the rooms.

The deck above them creaked. Both of them tilted their heads. Could be the wind buffeting the dilapidated structure. The old boat had all sorts of creaking and groaning going on.

Maybe it had been a mistake to come down here. Still, it seemed like the best way to shake or subdue their pursuer.

More creaking surrounded them, and then the distinct tapping of footsteps above them indicated someone was on deck. Joseph's gaze darted around the room. In a little alcove that had probably been a pantry, he spotted a tarp and pieces of wood.

More footsteps above them.

He ran over and lifted the tarp. She slipped under. He piled some boards on top to make it look haphazard. Then he nestled in beside Sierra.

"We only take him if we have to," he said. The better scenario would be for the assassin to give up. Taking the man out meant Joseph's cover might be blown.

They were squeezed into the tight space, their shoulders pressing against each other's. He could hear her breathing in the dark. Not much light got below deck this time of night. As far as he knew, the pursuer didn't have a flashlight with him.

The pursuer's footsteps echoed as he moved through the belowdeck rooms.

Dust filled Joseph's nose, causing a tickling sensation.

The footsteps drew closer. The pursuer was in the galley. There was a scratching sound and then more footsteps as the man moved around the room.

Joseph closed his eyes and counted. If he thought about how badly he wanted to sneeze, it would only make things worse. The gentle expansion and collapse of Sierra's body where it pressed against him stopped. She must be holding her breath.

The man took several steps toward them. His feet scratched the dirty floor as if he was turning in a circle.

Silence descended like a shroud. Joseph didn't dare even swallow for fear of being found. Every muscle in his body tensed. He was ready to jump the guy if he had to.

The man let out a humph noise, and then his footsteps retreated. They waited, still as statues, silent as the night while the footsteps clapped the boards below deck and then creaked above them.

They waited squeezed together in the tight space, not daring to move. Sierra's hair smelled like the lake. Their damp shoulders touched.

Minutes passed. He lifted his gaze upward. Was the man perched outside, ready to pounce on them once they emerged one by one?

Sierra twitched. She let out a breath. "I think he's gone," she whispered.

He moved away from her and pulled the tarp from his face. The hiding place had not been a great one. He was still concerned that the man was watching the boat. Maybe he didn't want to take on both of them at once in a closed space. For whatever reason, his primary target seemed to be Sierra. Why?

He wondered if she was as innocent as she seemed. A lot of violence in the drug trade was over turf wars.

If she was involved, maybe he could get her to flip, give up some information. The fact that he'd saved her life gave him leverage. But now was not the time to deal with that. He needed to make sure they had truly gotten rid of their assassin.

Joseph cupped her shoulder. "I'll go up first and let you know when the coast is clear."

She nodded.

He stepped lightly over the debris and floor-boards and then eased up the steps that led to the deck. Once on deck, he crouched behind a pile of rope and boards. He scanned the area around the boat. Moonlight washed over it, but the surrounding area was covered in shadows. He stuck his head back down the hole that led below deck. "Clear."

The stairs creaked as Sierra made her way up. She stepped on deck and scooted up beside him. They scurried to the edge of the boat. Joseph climbed down the rope ladder first. He waited below while Sierra made her way to the ground.

He pivoted one way and then the other, still listening, still on high alert.

Sierra's body banged against the boat. She hung on to the broken rope ladder as it swung back and forth. To her credit, she hadn't screamed, but the noise when she'd hit the boat would have alerted anyone close by.

"I got you." He reached up, wrapping his hands around her legs and allowing her to slide to the ground as his hands steadied her.

They stood facing each other. His hands were still on her waist. She was close enough for him to feel her breath on his neck. "Sorry," she whispered.

"It's not your fault it broke. It's worn out."

He let go of her and turned, staring out into the brush. "I don't think he would give up so easily. He's probably watching the road, thinking that's the most likely direction for us to go."

She pulled her phone out of her pocket and pressed a couple of buttons. "My phone is ruined from being soaked."

He took his phone out, as well. "I'm sure mine is, too." He stared at the black screen and touched the keypad. Nothing. He'd had it turned off, not wanting to risk it ringing while he was on surveillance. "You know this area better than I do."

She crossed her arms over her chest. "I have a friend whose cabin isn't too far from here. She lets me take kids up there."

"Is there a phone?"

"No, but we can get dried out and eat something. She has some mountain bikes. It will take longer, but we can take the trails back into town. It's certainly not the way anyone would predict us to get back home."

He nodded. "Okay. We'll do that." Now was as good a time as any to figure out where she was coming from. "You want to tell me why that guy was after you?"

She lifted her chin. "As soon as you tell me why you were out there when a drug deal was about to go down."

He caught the note of challenge in her voice. Trust between them was tenuous at best.

He wasn't going to get any information out of her just yet. She was still too defensive and suspicious of him. "Let's hike to that cabin."

"It should take less than half an hour to get there," she said.

Joseph kept pace with Sierra as they made their way along the shore. Even though he had protected her from harm, it was clear she still thought he was up to something.

He didn't know what to make of her, either. Was she telling the truth about being out there to help a kid? One thing he knew for sure—he had to protect his cover. If she found out who he really was, it could cost him his life.

THREE

Sierra hurried along the beach. Her friend's cabin was set back from the shore, nestled in some trees. The terrain around this part of the lake was more treacherous and not as developed as it was closer to town.

She was determined to find out what Joseph's involvement was with those two men. Was he a rival drug dealer, and it somehow benefited him to keep her alive? That assumption didn't seem to fit his gentle demeanor.

They entered a forested area. She sprinted along a path that could barely be called a trail. The cabin, surrounded by trees, came into view. Her friend had wanted a place that was low profile to get away to write and pray.

It must have been three or four in the morning. The sun wouldn't be up for another couple of hours.

The cabin was primitive, with only a generator for electricity. She found the key hidden in the coffee can behind a bush. She pushed the door open and glanced back at Joseph. He looked like he'd been dragged behind a truck.

She touched her own hair self-consciously. She probably looked just as bad.

He stared down at his muddy shirt. "Yeah, neither of us is exactly ready for prom night."

She laughed. He'd picked up on what she was thinking without her having to say anything. He had a nice smile…whoever he was.

She gritted her teeth. Was all that charm just to lure kids into the dark world of drugs? She hoped not.

She stepped inside. "I'll build a fire. There should be some canned goods in the cupboard."

Though her clothes had dried out somewhat, she still felt soggy and chilled. Within minutes, the fire sparked to life and heat filled the room. She collapsed in one of the overstuffed chairs that faced the fire.

Joseph spoke to her from the kitchen. "Looks like there's beans and peaches. Unless you want me to heat something up."

She touched her growling stomach. "Anything would be nice." She closed her eyes, feeling like she might cry. Because they welcomed at-risk kids into youth group, she was used to sticky situations. She had seen her own share of violence when she'd stepped into the dark world of drug use. She wanted to help these kids the way she had been helped all those years ago. But she'd never had her life threatened like it had been tonight.

Joseph moved around the kitchen opening and shutting cupboards. The kitchen was only partially visible from where she sat.

He emerged holding two glasses of water. "Thought you might be thirsty."

She took the glass. He sat down in the other chair and stared at the fire, twisting the glass of water in his hand. "There's a little cookstove in there. I'll heat something up for us. If you like, I can make you a warm cup of tea."

His kindness seemed so genuine. Was he buttering her up for some reason? Drug dealers were good at winning people over. She supposed if he had wanted to harm her, though, he would have done it by now.

She took a sip of her water. The cool liquid traveled down her throat and splashed in her empty stomach. She tilted the glass and took a bigger swallow. "Hot food and tea sounds really good. Let me catch my breath and I'll help you."

He gulped down his water.

Her muscles were heavy with fatigue, and she longed for sleep.

Joseph held the empty glass and stared at the fire. "Some crazy night, huh?"

She glanced over at him. She could see why all the teen girls had a crush on him. He was tall. The sun had created honey-colored highlights in his brown wavy, shoulder-length hair. His brown eyes were the color of dark chocolate, and his voice held just the hint of a Southern accent. His skin was deeply tanned. He looked like a surfer who had gotten lost on the way to the coast.

She could feel herself becoming guarded. His question was meant to open up a conversation. He was probing for information for some reason. "Yeah, it was a crazy night."

He straightened in his chair and stared at the floor for a long moment. "I don't know what you think about me. But please believe me, I don't want you to come to any harm."

He had pulled her from danger more than once. And though he'd had an opportunity to harm her, he had kept her safe. "Okay, I'll give you that."

He turned to face her. "Why were you out there?"

She watched his unwavering gaze as a tiny bit of trust grew inside her.

"Like I said, I was out there to get a kid. I talked him out of getting involved with the drug trade. I'm not sure why he ran. I'm worried about his safety, but I'm also concerned that he decided to throw in with the drug dealers after all. Those dealers must have shown up early. I thought I had time to get him out."

Why would he ask the same question over and over, expecting a different answer? That sort of questioning technique was something a cop would do. Was it possible Joseph was on the other side of the law?

"Do you know why the guy in the baseball hat tried to strangle and drown you?"

Yeah, he was definitely acting like a cop. Her whole body convulsed when the memory of nearly dying rose to the surface. She wrapped her arms over her chest.

Joseph reached out and touched her arm. "You're safe now." He rubbed her forearm in a soothing way. His touch calmed her. His kindness seemed to break down even more walls.

Joseph put his empty glass on the wood floor. The fire in the fireplace crackled.

She took in a breath, appreciating that he waited until she was ready to talk. "That second man, the one who came out on shore and then disappeared into the trees when we were in the boat—"

"I didn't get a good look at him. I was trying to start the boat."

"I saw him earlier in the forest." A chill penetrated her skin. "He had drugs in a satchel. He was holding a brick in his hand."

Joseph sat up a little straighter. "Really? What else do you remember about him?"

"Not a lot. Getting shot at kind of wipes things from your memory." She touched her own wrist. "He had this big gold watch on the hand that held the brick."

Joseph leaned toward her, his eyes growing wide. "You think you would recognize him?"

She still shuddered at the memory. So much trauma had happened since that moment. She tried to recall the man's features. "I think if I saw him again I might." She rose to her feet. "You ask a lot of questions for a guy who runs a skateboard shop." And carried a gun.

He shrugged. "That other guy seemed bent on your destruction. I was trying to figure out why it was happening…if it will keep happening until that guy is behind bars."

She paced as anxiety caused her to tense up. The man she'd seen in the forest must be important to the drug trade. Even when they got safely back to town, her life might be in danger. "I should go to the police. They have files, photographs of drug dealers. If I saw him again, maybe it would jog my memory. I got an even closer look at the guy with the baseball hat."

Joseph didn't respond.

Every time she mentioned the police, Joseph fell silent. Old suspicions rose to the surface.

The words she'd just spoken settled around her. This was all too much. She rested her palm against her face.

Joseph's voice was filled with compassion as he rose to his feet. "You're going to be okay."

"Meaning that I'll be left alone, right?" She shook her head, still trying to fathom what all this meant.

Joseph squeezed her hand. "Why don't you sit? I'll go heat us up some water and food. Then we'll be back on our way to Scenic View."

He hadn't answered her question. "I'll have to leave a note for my friend so she doesn't think elves came in and raided her pantry and took her bikes."

Sierra closed her eyes and listened to Joseph bustling around in the kitchen. He was still being evasive with her. She tensed. More than anything, she wanted to believe that the violence of the night was an isolated incident and that she would be able to go back to life as normal.

Predawn light warmed Joseph's face as they pedaled the mountain bikes down the trail that led back into Scenic View. The food had revived him somewhat, but he was beyond exhausted, and he had to open the shop in a few hours so he could keep up appearances of being a mild-mannered store manager.

Sierra was talking about going to the police. If one of the local cops was feeding info to the drug network, it could put Sierra in even more danger. He had a choice to make. Could he trust her enough to let her in on his cover and tell her why they needed to leave the police out of this? She probably suspected already that he wasn't who he said he was.

He stopped on the flat part of the trail to catch his breath. Sierra followed ten yards behind him. She rounded the hill and sailed down the trail toward him.

Sierra braked beside him and brushed her hair out of her eyes. She was pretty in an unconventional way. The thin nose and slanted eyes made her look fragile, like a porcelain doll. He admired Sierra. Whatever suspicions she harbored about Trevor, it was clear she cared about him and the other kids she worked with.

In the distance, the outskirts of Scenic View were visible. The resort hotel built on the lakefront towered over everything. There were only a few boats on the lake at this early hour. Washed in the warm glow of early morning light, the water shimmered.

Mention of the large-faced gold watch led Joseph to believe Sierra had seen the man DEA had been tracking for years, a dangerous man who would go to all lengths not to be identified, judging from the way the man in the base-ball hat had gone after her. He had a feeling he should stick close to her for her protection. She could help with his investigation, but not if something happened to her.

"So, do you have a job you need to get to?"

She shook her head. "I work from home. I'm a bookkeeper."

"You mind hanging out at the shop until we're sure this whole thing has blown over?"

She glanced at him, and he saw the fear behind her eyes. "I'm still worried about Trevor. I at least need to make some calls and tell the police he's missing."

"Why don't you start by calling around from the shop?"

She shrugged and then her expression grew pensive. "I can't live my life like a captive. I'll just go to the police. They can help me."

"Sure, I suppose." He didn't need the local cops sniffing around him or his shop. He pushed off on the bike. "I'm sure we can work something out."

The wheels whirred up and down the hills until the landscape flattened out and they came to the edge of town. This was an older part of town. The houses were built on bigger lots but were more run-down.

In his short time living here, the town seemed

to be a place of contrast. Between rich and lower class. Between old and showy.

The drug problem here was bad and had escalated in recent months. Both bored kids with disposable incomes looking for a thrill and kids trapped in the cycle of poverty were targets. Scenic View was believed to be the hub for drug distribution throughout the Northwest.

They pedaled down the street.

Joseph swung around to the alley of the skateboard shop. He lived in the apartment above the shop. After opening the lower level of the shop so they could push the bikes in to keep them from being stolen, he headed up the stairs. Sierra followed behind him.

He opened the door and stepped inside, hurrying to pick up some workout clothes he'd left on the couch. Glancing around, he realized that his place looked like a total bachelor pad, with dishes in the sink and sports equipment piled in the corner. Why did it matter to him what she thought of his place?

He scooted a box of his stuff out of the way, laughing nervously. "Still haven't finished unpacking."

"It's nice. Cozy," she said. "And your commute time to work is close to perfect."

He pointed for her to sit down on the couch. "If you don't mind, I'd like to get a couple hours' sleep before I have to open up the shop." Once his clerk came in, he would have to retrieve his boat. "Why don't we wait on contacting the police. I can stick close to you for a little while until we know that guy won't be after you anymore." Though he didn't want to alarm her—Sierra could potentially identify a man they'd been tracking for years—chances were, her life was still in danger.

She studied him for a moment. "I could use some rest, I guess."

He hurried over to a closet and pulled out a blanket. "Be my guest. Take the couch."

"Do you have a landline? I want to make a few calls about Trevor first," she said.

"In the kitchen." If she didn't locate Trevor, she'd probably call the police about him. He couldn't see the harm in that—the kid needed to be found—as long as she didn't get the cops poking around his life and figuring out he was undercover.

Joseph stepped down the hallway and collapsed on his bed. He listened to Sierra's soft voice as she talked on the phone. His jaw tensed. He walked a tightrope here. Sierra was going to need some level of protection. If she knew he was undercover, they could come up with a ruse as to why they were together. She was working for him. Or they were an item.

Out in the living room, things had gone silent. She must have lain down to sleep.

Joseph pulled a pay-as-you-go phone out of his bureau drawer. His work required that he always keep an extra around. He dialed a number and explained the situation to his handler.

"It is your call. If you think you can trust her not to blow your cover," said the handler. "Clearly, she's important to the investigation. Maybe her memory would be jogged if we got her to sit down with a sketch artist."

"I think I can trust her." He clicked the phone off and closed his eyes. It took him only minutes to drift off to sleep.

Sometime later, the ringing of the phone woke him with a start. He heard Sierra's voice, this time filled with panic as she talked.

She must have given his number to the people she'd called about Trevor. His chest squeezed tight. Judging from the tone of her voice, something bad had happened.

Sierra couldn't believe what she was hearing. "Trevor, where are you?"

"I'm in trouble, Miss M. You need to come and get me. I can't explain. I'm at Leman's junkyard. Please hurry." The line went dead.

She hung up the phone with a trembling hand.

Was Trevor's plea sincere, or was she being set up? The anguish in his voice seemed very real.

Joseph spoke from the hallway where he stood. "What's going on?"

"It's Trevor. He's in trouble." She turned to face him. "I need to go get him."

"How did he know to call my number?"

"I gave this number out to the people I called when I was looking for him. He must have gotten in touch with one of them first." She rested her palm on her chest, where her heart beat erratically. "I have to go."

"This could be a setup."

"I know. I also know Trevor's character and how hard he worked to get sober. I couldn't live with myself if he was sincere and I left him out to dry."

"It could be a dangerous situation. Why don't you let me go?"

"Trevor trusts me."

"I'm going with you, then," Joseph said. "You don't have a car, anyway."

"I could just borrow yours." Relief mixed with guilt as she stared into Joseph's brown eyes. "What about the shop?" The truth was, she would feel better having Joseph's help. She was still shaken by their run through the forest and being shot at.

"I can call my clerk and tell him to come in

early and open up." He grabbed a denim jacket off the rack where he hung his coats. "Take this. Looks like a chilly morning out there." He left the room and returned a moment later, wearing a jacket and holding a phone.

"Do you always keep a spare phone around?"

He grinned. "It's a Boy Scout thing. Always be prepared." Then he pressed in some numbers on the phone and pointed toward the landline phone. "Make note of the number Trevor called from the caller ID."

When she checked the number, she realized it wasn't Trevor's regular number. More cause for alarm. She wrote it down. Sierra listened while Joseph spoke to the clerk. Nothing in his tone let on that they were facing an urgent situation. "Listen, Jake, something has come up. If you could come in half an hour early and open up the shop, that would be great."

Joseph listened for a moment and then said, "Okay, thanks." He hung up the phone and gazed at Sierra.

His eyes seemed to look right through her. There was something he wasn't saying. He hurried down the hallway and returned a moment later without explanation. They headed out the door, down to his Jeep.

She tensed.

What if they were stepping into a trap?

She still didn't know why Trevor had run off down at Fisherman's Crest. She didn't know where the boy's loyalties lay. But she did know that she had to give the kid the benefit of the doubt, if there was any chance at all for him to turn his life around. Last night and this morning, when she'd talked to him on the phone, she'd detected the anguish in his voice.

Joseph twisted the key in the ignition. "You're going to have to give me directions."

"Head toward the north side of town. Take a left off State Street and follow the road out of town."

"Easy peasy," said Joseph.

She appreciated how calm he seemed to be. It helped her to relax, as well, as the morning sun warmed the interior of the car. Maybe this would just be a simple pickup. Sometimes teenagers tended to be dramatic when there was no reason to be.

She glanced over at Joseph as they came to the edge of town. He drove past fields filled with cows, and the road changed from gravel to dirt. They drove for a long time without seeing another dwelling. This place was pretty remote.

Then the junkyard, surrounded by a high fence, came into view. Buses and single-wide trailers served as part of the fence. The man who had owned the junkyard, Peter Leman, had died two years before, leaving no heirs. The county had not had the funds to clean up the area. The No Trespassing signs had not stopped teens from using it as a place to hang out.

"The front gate is locked. We'll have to park outside and walk in."

Joseph pulled off the road and killed the engine. "This is a big place."

"I have a pretty good idea where he might be." She pushed open her door. "There's a gap in the fence where we can get in."

As she hurried around to the side of the junkyard, her heartbeat kicked up several notches. She slipped in between a bus and board fence.

Joseph followed her. He stood beside her, his hand slipped into his open jacket. She saw then why he had gone into the bedroom. He had a gun in a shoulder holster. He thought they might be stepping into something violent, too.

Hadn't he lost his first gun somewhere on their run through the forest? Maybe it was just for protecting his business, but she wondered why the manager of a skateboard shop would have two guns.

A wall of partially crushed cars blocked her view of the rest of the junkyard. "This place is an accident waiting to happen, but we haven't been able to keep the kids from coming here." Sierra maneuvered around the wall of cars.

"I don't get it. Scenic View has all kinds of recreational possibilities. Why come here?"

"I think it's the danger factor. Didn't you like adrenaline when you were a teenager?"

"Still do." He offered her a brief smile, raising his eyebrows.

The moment of humor that passed between them lightened the tension she felt. She zigzagged through the junkyard, past rows of appliances and piles of tires. There were several sheds on the property that Sierra knew contained old books, magazines and newspapers. Peter Leman had been the ultimate hoarder.

Joseph tilted his head to look up at a mountain of twisted and intertwined pieces of metal. He shook his head. "It's like an amusement park for junk collectors."

"There is a big pipe at the far end of the fence where kids hang out." She glanced around, not seeing any signs of anyone else in the junkyard.

As they made their way through the labyrinth of junk, wind blew around them, causing the metal to creak. Tarps that covered piles of junk flapped in the wind.

She pointed. "The pipe is just on the other side of that motor home."

He crouched by the motor home. She slipped in behind him, unsure what was going on here.

A hundred frantic thoughts zinged through Sierra's head. Was Trevor safe? Was he even here?

Had the drug dealers set him up to make the call, or had his emergency been an emotional one? Had he decided to ally himself with the dealers after all?

Again, Joseph touched his chest where the gun was. "Let's take this slow."

His action sent a fresh dose of terror through her. He was anticipating violence.

FOUR

Joseph pulled his gun and rushed toward the next object that would provide them with cover, in case someone was lying in wait for them in the pipe. He crouched behind a pile of car doors, then lifted his head above them. He could not see the interior of the pipe, but it was easily big enough for a grown person to stand inside.

Though arguing with Sierra about coming out here would have been an act of futility, he still didn't like the idea of putting her or any civilian in danger.

She'd handled herself fine while they had been running from the drug dealer by the lake. He wondered what made her so tenacious in her need to help this messed-up kid who might have betrayed her.

Sierra leaned close to Joseph's ear and whispered, "Should I call out for him?"

Joseph shook his head. What if someone more

dangerous than Trevor was close by? "You stay here. Let me go."

She nodded.

With his gun lifted, he ran toward the pipe. The interior came into view. He lowered his gun. There was no one inside, only evidence of what went on there—empty beer bottles and even a syringe. A magazine lay open, its pages flapping in the breeze.

The sight of the debris, of lives being destroyed, made his heart heavy. His baby brother, Ezra, had been so young when he'd overdosed. How did someone with so much to live for get to such a hopeless, dark place?

Sierra came up behind him. She must have sensed his shift in mood. "You all right?"

He pointed inside the pipe, backing away from the memories of Ezra's transformation from a happy, bright kid to a prisoner of his own addiction. "This kind of stuff makes me angry." Very few people knew why he had become a DEA agent. The pain still cut deep.

"Me, too," she said. Her expression softened, and her voice filled with compassion. "I just decide every day, in whatever small way I can, I'll work to pull a kid from the fire before he or she is consumed."

He studied her for a long moment, feeling drawn to her. "Exactly." They were on the same side. Both of them fighting for the same thing, just in different ways.

They searched the rest of the junkyard, finding no one or any evidence that someone had been here recently. When he tried the number Trevor had called from, the phone didn't even ring on the other end.

"Probably a throwaway phone," he said.

Frustrated, he slipped outside the junkyard and returned to his car. Sierra followed him. She sat in the passenger seat while he settled in behind the steering wheel and buckled his seat belt.

"Something is going on with Trevor. He sounded scared on that phone call. We have to find him." She laced her fingers together. Her forehead furrowed.

His heart went out to her. "We need some kind of lead to find him. Kids talk when they come into the shop. They think I'm not listening. And some of them even trust me enough to let me know what they know."

She turned to face him. "Yes, the skateboard shop is ideal for finding out what's going on with teenagers. Even the ones who are using drugs." She narrowed her eyes at him, expecting a response.

This was the moment of truth. "I guess you figured it out."

"You didn't act like a shop owner back there in the junkyard. You acted like a cop."

He tensed. "It's important that no one else know."

"I'm good at keeping secrets." A soft smile graced her lips.

"That man you saw in the forest is very high up in the drug trade." He placed his hands on the steering wheel. "If we can take him down, it would go a long way to destroying the drug network in this area."

"So that's why he sent his henchman after me." Her voice filled with anxiety.

He turned the key in the ignition and pressed the gas. He wished there was something he could say to lift the burden of worry from her. Sometimes silence was the kinder choice over saying something trite or untrue.

The car rolled up a long hill. "Kind of like a roller-coaster ride," he said, hoping to distract her from her worry. He aimed the car downhill and coasted, lifting his foot off the gas.

"Yeah, I guess. Never thought of it that way." She sounded a million miles away as she stared through the windshield.

The car picked up speed. Joseph pressed the brakes, but the car rolled even faster.

So that's why they'd been lured out there.

The brake line had been cut.

* * *

Sierra's pulse raced as she watched Joseph's expression change. His features hardened with concern as he pumped the brakes.

He applied the emergency brake, but that didn't seem to make a difference.

She didn't need to ask him what was wrong. They were traveling at a dangerous speed on a dirt road. This was a long downhill. Before the road leveled off, they ran the risk of the car flipping.

Sierra gripped the armrest.

Joseph stared straight ahead and clutched the steering wheel, keeping the car to the center of the road. There was a ditch on one side. The gravel at the edges of the road could function like marbles, causing the car to roll over.

Her heart raced, and every muscle in her body turned to stone as they hurtled downhill. The road leveled off a little, but the car kept rolling.

Joseph turned the wheel. The car caught air as they sailed over the ditch. She saw now what his plan was. The field beside the road contained round hay bales. Joseph steered toward one but turned abruptly.

"Still going too fast," he said, steering around another hay bale. The car bumped over the uneven terrain as the scenery through the window went by in a blur.

"This is it," he said through gritted teeth.

She looked away as the hay bale filling the windshield drew ever closer. The impact jerked her forward and then back. The car was too old for air bags. The seat belt dug into her skin. The wind had been knocked out of her. She wheezed in a sharp, trembling breath.

The entire car seemed to vibrate from the impact. Metal creaked and groaned.

She opened her eyes.

Joseph put his hand on her shoulder. "You okay?"

She wondered if she was as pale as Joseph. Her body felt like it was being shaken from the inside out.

She cleared her throat, trying to answer, but managed only a nod.

"Stay put." He pushed open his door.

She stared through the windshield, which was 90 percent hay bale with only a sliver of blue sky visible. Her hands trembled, and her stomach felt like it had sustained a blow.

Joseph opened her door. He reached across her and unclicked her seat belt. Gently, he took her arm and lifted her up. She collapsed against his chest.

The run through the night, the worry over what was going on with Trevor and the accident had taken its toll on her. She thought of herself as a strong woman, but this was all too much. Joseph must have seen it in her expression. He held her for a long moment. She rested her head against his chest, squeezing her eyes tight to keep from crying. Her face brushed against the soft fabric of his cotton shirt. Finally, she stopped shaking and could take in a deep breath.

She stepped away from the warmth of his embrace, embarrassed that she had fallen apart. "Sorry, I'm just not used to all this." She pulled a strand of hair off her face and touched her fingers to her lips.

"I'm impressed with how well you held it together." He squeezed her arm just above the elbow and offered her a faint smile.

She appreciated his effort at calming her, but she was having a hard time accepting what had just happened. "You don't think those brakes just stopped working because of wear and tear."

He shook his head. "The car is too bent for me to check the brake line, even if it wasn't stuck in a hay bale." He looked back at the car. "We won't know until we have it looked at, but my guess is we were set up."

His conclusion sent a fresh wave of fear through her and made her wonder again about Trevor's innocence.

Joseph opened his door and pulled out his phone. "Might as well get a tow truck out here."

Neither of them spoke for several minutes. This was her new reality. Being hunted and sabotaged.

"These guys play for keeps." Her voice held a note of terror. "What do I do now? Go to the police?"

"Not the local cops. We think one of them might be connected to the drug trade."

Not sure how to respond, Sierra let that news sink in. She knew most of the city police. Some of them she had gone to high school with. "What makes you say that?"

"I'm not the first undercover guy to come to this area. In the past, anytime we involved the locals, the investigation fell apart. I know this kind of relentless violence must be hard for you." Joseph stopped. He shifted his weight from one foot to the other and then stared at his phone. "Let me make this call so we can get back to town."

She crossed her arms over her chest and paced while Joseph made the call. As he talked, giving the tow truck driver their location, she could feel a sense of resolve growing inside her even as she battled with her own fear. She held an important piece to a puzzle and could give kids, the kids she worked with, a fighting chance at a decent life.

Joseph finished the call. "I want to help you as much as I can to put this guy away," Sierra said.

He locked her in his gaze. "You would put yourself at risk like that?"

"Yes. Years ago someone did that for me." She took in a breath. "A teacher who cared about me saved me from the druggie house I was staying at." Sharing this information about her past was always scary. "I need to pay it forward. I've seen what drugs do to the soul. If I can help even one kid, I have to do it."

A look of admiration spread across his face. "Well then, I guess you better hang close to me until we can figure out who that guy you saw in the forest was. If he has been arrested before, he'll be in our database."

There was no judgment in his demeanor, only acceptance. She felt closer to him in that moment, knowing that she had shared the most shameful thing about herself and he had not rejected her. "I know another dealer might take his place, but every one of those guys who gets put away means my kids are helped."

She stared out at the landscape and then out on the road. They had gone miles out of town. The tow truck driver wouldn't be here for at least twenty minutes. Though there were fields and cows, the farmhouse they belonged to could be miles from where they were. This area was pretty far from civilization.

Joseph glanced over his shoulder. His posture stiffened, sending a new wave of fear through her. He whirled around to face her, concern etched in his facial features.

Suddenly he tackled her. She fell to the ground just as the zing of a rifle shot filled the air.

Once he knew Sierra was out of the line of fire, he rolled free of her and crawled back toward the nearest hay bale. Hardly the best cover, but it was what they had to work with. A second shot shattered the silence around them. Still crouching low, he stumbled to his feet and darted toward the next hay bale with Sierra on his heels.

He grabbed Sierra's hand and pulled her to the far side of the bale.

Sierra spoke between breaths. "Where did that come from?"

"Truck at the top of the hill." The straw of the bale felt itchy against his back.

"They must have been behind us. When they saw we survived the car sabotage, they decided to finish the job." She put her palm on her chest.

"We can't wait for the tow truck driver. We'll have to head cross-country. Stay off the road." He looked directly at her. "Ready to make a run for the next hay bale?"

They darted from one hay bale to the next. Joseph looked over his shoulder. The truck had made its way down the hill and was headed toward the field. They couldn't outrun a truck.

"You keep going. I'll let him get close enough. See if I can take out his tires with my pistol." He pulled his gun from the shoulder holster.

She nodded and took off running. He watched her dive behind a hay bale before turning his attention back to the oncoming truck. He could see only one person behind the wheel, no passenger.

He crouched low and pressed against the hay bale. A handgun had decent accuracy at short distances. His heart pounded against his rib cage. The truck loomed closer. The roar of the motor seemed to surround him. He jumped up and took aim, hitting the front tire closest to him and then rolling free of the trajectory of the truck.

The truck stuttered but continued to roll forward. The driver turned his wheel and aimed right for him. Joseph stood and took a second shot at the other front tire. The bullet zinged off metal.

He'd missed. Then he aimed a third shot through the windshield, not to kill but to disorient.

The truck came to a stop as the driver picked up his rifle and pointed through the shattered windshield.

Joseph dropped to the ground and rolled toward a rusty metal trough. Once he had some cover, he lifted his head and lined up a shot to go through the other front tire. He pulled the trigger, then burst to his feet, not taking time to see if he'd hit his target.

His legs pumped as the fear of death energized him. He sprinted toward the next hay bale. A rifle shot zinged through the air, but it was aimed toward Sierra, who was running for the cover of a cluster of trees. He breathed in a quick wordless prayer for her safety.

Joseph dove behind a hay bale and pressed his back against it. He peered around to see the shooter stalking toward him. The man wore a different colored baseball hat pulled low over his face, but he had the same build as the man who had come after them down by the lake.

Joseph glanced in the direction Sierra had run, making his way toward the trees. He entered the trees and came out on the other side. The hay field ended and the land sloped upward.

He spotted Sierra ahead, running toward the road. She slowed when she looked back and saw him. He put his gun back into the shoulder holster and headed toward her.

The land reconnected with the road. Sierra waited for him, resting her hands on her knees to catch her breath. He met up with her, glancing down to where he had just been. The shooter emerged from the cluster of trees.

Sierra's eyes grew wide when she followed the line of his gaze.

Both of them crouched and headed toward the far side of the road, where there was a ditch. A rifle shot stirred up dirt on the road and pummeled his eardrum.

Staying low, they crawled along in the ditch.

In the morning light, he could see the outskirts of Scenic View and the lake shimmering in the distance. Though cutting across the field had brought them closer to town, it had to be a long jog to get to the edge of town, longer if they had to dodge bullets and stay off the road. He doubted the shooter wanted witnesses, so once they were around people or on a part of the road where there was traffic, they'd be safe. Or maybe they could flag down the tow truck when it came.

Sierra was still breathless from running. "We can cut across country. Head through that field there." She pointed toward a barbed wire fence where cows grazed and plodded around.

She knew the countryside better than he did. He followed her lead, slipping through the barbed wire and climbing over. When he looked back, he didn't see the shooter.

"Pick a cow," he said.

He rushed over to a black heifer who chewed away at a tuft of grass. He lined his feet up with the cow's back feet so they wouldn't be spotted. He'd been a DEA agent for nearly ten years. In all that time, there had never been a training exercise in which they had to use livestock for cover. Despite the danger they still faced, something about that struck him as funny. He smiled and shook his head as he ran to hide behind another slow-moving cow.

Sierra darted behind a cow shelter, a three-sided wood structure. Joseph lifted his head just above the cow's back, stepping sideways as the cow ambled toward some grass. The shooter paced up and down along the road, looking out across the field and then up the road, clearly confused as to which way he and Sierra had gone.

Joseph heard the rumble of a truck engine in the distance. The tow truck he'd called came into view around a curve. The shooter darted off the road and headed toward the cluster of trees, probably not wanting to be spotted.

The driver was going too fast to give Joseph

time to get up to the road and flag it down. He watched the tow truck disappear around another curve. They couldn't get back to their wrecked car without being shot at. The shooter blocked that path to safety. He was in the cluster of trees between the road where the tow truck had gone and where they were. The tow truck's appearance bought him and Sierra valuable seconds when they would not be shot at. He ran toward the cow shelter where Sierra waited. If they crouched and ran in a straight line, the shelter would keep them from being spotted.

He held his hand out to Sierra. Her fingers gripped his as she pulled herself to her feet. He locked her in his gaze as her touch sent an electric charge through him.

"Stay low. I think we can make it back into town," he said.

Fatigue settled into his muscles as he made his way to the edge of the field and climbed through the barbed wire fence. Sierra seemed to be tiring, too. They cut across country through an aspen grove.

He stopped, leaning against a tree and looking over his shoulder. No sign of the shooter. Sierra pressed her back against a tree and slid to the ground. Even though weariness was evident in her features and she was muddy from their run through the field, he was drawn to the light he saw in her eyes and the way her mouth turned up in a faint smile.

She rested her head against the tree trunk and let out a heavy breath. "That was something." Her expression grew serious. "I suppose we shouldn't stay here for long."

"I don't see him, but yes, we can't take any chances."

She pushed herself to her feet. Her blue eyes studied. "Let's get moving, then."

The green aspen's leaves shimmered like coins in the morning light, making a melodic rustling sound in the breeze. His heart beat a little faster when she looked at him. Sierra had shown herself to be a brave, quick-thinking woman. "You do okay for a bookkeeper." He reached over and pulled a piece of straw out of her silky dark hair.

The gesture seemed to make her aware of her appearance as she brushed her dark hair off her face and then looked away. "Thanks." Color rose up in her cheeks.

He pulled himself free from the moment of attraction and angled his body around the trees. The shooter was making his way across the field, slowed by having to carry the rifle but tenacious in pursuit of his prey.

Joseph's heart revved up a notch. His muscles tensed, ready for fight or flight. "Let's get going. I'm calling the tow truck driver to see if he can pick us up on his way back into town. The shooter has made it clear he doesn't want to be spotted." He glanced back over his shoulder. "In the meantime, let's keep moving."

The trees provided them with a degree of cover as they rushed toward town and safety. Maybe they would get away this time, but he knew it would just be a matter of hours before the assassin came after Sierra again.

FIVE

Sierra sipped her warm cup of tea and clicked through the photographs on the computer screen. She studied one mug shot after another. None of them looked like the man with the satchel or the one who had come after them so relentlessly. The photographs of the men, scarred, tattooed, glaring at the camera lens, sent a shiver down her spine. Her addiction had taken her only to the perimeter of that violent world.

The skateboard shop buzzed with late-day activity while Joseph unpacked boxes of inventory and jumped in to help his teenage clerk, Jake, when needed. They had caught a ride from the tow truck and spent the day together in the shop.

Joseph had suggested that she stay in the shop until closing, so he could keep an eye on her and get her some additional protection. He couldn't be with her all the time because he needed to maintain his cover as a shop owner.

She watched as Joseph joked with his teen-age clerk, giving him a friendly punch on the shoulder. He had probably seen the darkest side of human nature in his job. Yet he was kind.

When she was just sixteen, she'd fallen for a nineteen-year-old boy who had seen the wound in her from her messed-up family life and drawn her into the world of drugs. She admired Joseph, liked him even, but she didn't trust herself where men were concerned. The best thing for her to do was to pour her energy into the teens she wanted to help.

She took another sip of tea, appreciating the warmth as it traveled down her throat. Besides, Joseph probably came from a solid family, not one like hers. Parents divorced, her mother dead from an overdose of pills, her father married to a much younger woman he had had an affair with.

"Hey, Miss M. What are you doing here?"

She looked up from the computer screen and closed the laptop. Thirteen-year-old Ginny, with her freckles and red hair, looked bright as sunshine to Sierra just now.

Joseph stopped unpacking a box of knee pads and eased toward them, probably tuning in to the conversation.

She couldn't exactly say she was looking at mug shots. "I'm doing the books for Mr. Anderson." She met Joseph's gaze. "He's great at running the shop, but his paperwork is a tangled mess."

Joseph offered her a faint smile. "Math and organization were never my thing," he said as he arranged the display of knee pads.

"Ginny, have you seen or heard from Trevor recently?"

The teenager shook her head. "I haven't seen him since group last week. Why?"

"I'm just worried about him."

She shrugged. "Does Daisy know where he is?"

"I talked to his sister this morning. Neither she nor his foster mom have seen him." Trevor's foster mom had already notified the police that he was missing.

Something across the room caught Ginny's attention, and she excused herself. Jake slipped into the back room to leave for his break.

Joseph leaned against the counter. "It wouldn't be a bad idea, you know."

"Me doing your books?"

"I'm not really a store manager, and I don't play one on TV." Joseph spoke under his breath. He leaned a little closer to her. "I just know how to act the part. I've been tossing my receipts in a box."

She let out a little laugh. "I suppose all the computer stuff isn't in one clearly labeled file."

"It wouldn't make people wonder why we are together," Joseph said.

All the customers including Ginny had left the shop.

"I'd like to leave this place in working order when all is said and done," Joseph said.

His comment sent a barb of pain through her heart. Joseph wasn't going to stay in Scenic View forever.

She glanced around the shop. His comment reminded her that all of this was just a front. Joseph would be gone as soon as the investigation was closed. They had been through so much in less than twenty-four hours. She was starting to feel a bond with him.

"You could work here in the shop," he added.

"You've only been in charge a short time. I suppose that would be a few days' work."

"You can bring your work for your other clients until I can figure out how to keep you safe." Though there was no one else in the shop, he spoke in a whisper.

His comment sent a new wave of fear through her. "I guess that will work as a temporary arrangement." She flipped open the laptop and continued to go through the photos.

He slipped around to the other side of the counter and squeezed her arm. "The shop is quiet. I'm going to make some calls. See what we can put into place for you as far as additional protection goes."

While she scanned through the photographs, she could hear Joseph on his cell phone talking in a low tone behind the closed door.

Face after face whizzed by on the computer screen. Her gaze froze on the face of the man who had tried to drown her, the man in the baseball hat. A chill skittered over her skin and sank down into her bones. He had a distinctive face. His features were all sharp angles, and he had pockmarks on his cheeks.

When she closed her eyes, the other man, the one with the watch, was harder to picture. Joseph had said he had a computer program that might help her combine different facial features to jar her memory. She filed through some more pictures. There had been something distinctive about the man. It was less about his physical features and more about the way he carried himself.

If she saw him again, she knew she would be able to identify him.

A rustling noise caused her to look up. A man with his back to her was looking at a display of skateboard wheels.

"Can I help you?"

The murmur of Joseph talking on the phone in the office had gone quiet. The man turned around and stalked toward her. "I don't know. Can you help me?"

Though the man smiled at her, his eyes were vacant pools. He must be a tourist or a newcomer. She didn't recognize him. He was a muscular man, built like a weight lifter, with big teeth.

Her heartbeat revved up a notch. Why did she sense danger? Was it just because of everything that had happened?

"Look, I'm just the bookkeeper. Why don't I go get the manager?" She turned to go.

The man reached across the counter and grabbed her hand, squeezing it. "Actually, it's you I want to talk to."

She tried to pull away. He pressed his fingers harder into her skin.

Perspiration formed on her forehead and her throat constricted. "Please, let me go get the manager."

He pulled her close, his face only inches from hers. "You just can't be too careful in this town, can you, Sierra?"

Her heart pounded. He knew her name.

He let go of her hand, pushing it across the counter. He turned and stalked toward the door.

Her knees were shaking as she rushed into the office. It was empty. There was another door that led outside. She rushed toward it and flung it open. Joseph stood in the alley watching several kids on skateboards do tricks.

He must have sensed her presence because he turned to look at her. "The kids knocked on my door and wanted to show me their new stuff." He stepped toward her, his smile fading as concern etched across his features. "Is everything all right?"

She opened her mouth to speak. Forming the words took substantial effort. "There was a man in the shop."

He rushed over to her and grabbed her hand. "Did he hurt you?"

She shook her head. His hand was warm where it touched hers. "He threatened me. He knew my name."

His expression hardened as he looked over her shoulder. "We might be able to catch him." He hurried back inside through the office to the storefront.

He had already stepped outside onto the sidewalk when Sierra caught up with him. He paced in one direction and then in the other. "Did you see what he was driving?" Joseph was like a wolf stalking his prey, intense and focused.

She placed her palm on her chest where her heart still raged as if she'd been sprinting. "No, I didn't see."

He shifted his focus to her. His voice grew softer. "Why don't we go back inside?"

Her knees still felt like cooked noodles. "I found the guy who came after us from your computer files. Baseball hat guy."

"That's a start." He put a protective hand on her upper back as they stepped into the shop.

"I went through all the pictures," she said. "I didn't see the man who had the drugs."

"Maybe he's not in the system," said Joseph. "He may be so elusive that he's never been arrested."

She was still having a hard time taking in a deep breath. "And I can go through the photos again to see if the man who was just here is in your files." The image of his face, his big teeth and sinister eyes, was burned into her mind.

"That's all good." Once inside, Joseph shoved his hand in his pockets and stared out the display window. His jaw was set tight. That man coming into his shop clearly upset him.

"I made some other calls. DEA can get a female agent here in a couple of days to stay with you at your house, if that works?"

"Sure, she can have the guest bedroom. The teens from group stay there from time to time." Though about half the kids she worked with came from fairly stable home situations, some were on the street, fighting with parents, trying to get clean or at odds with foster parents. Her house was a safe place for them to land until they could straighten out whatever problem they faced.

"Her cover is that she's a cousin visiting you for a while. If this thing stretches out, we'll set her up with a job and say that she decided to live here."

Sierra came and stood beside Joseph, staring out the window at the calm scene unfolding outside. Children played in the park across the street. A mom pushed a baby carriage. It felt as though a weight had been laid on her chest, making it hard to take in a deep breath. "If this thing stretches out?"

The words seemed to echo through her mind.

Joseph squeezed her shoulder. She looked up into his brown eyes. With his long, wavy hair, Hawaiian shirt and shorts, and laid-back attitude, she never would have guessed he was a cop. Maybe he played the part well because it was close to who he really was. She found herself wanting to get to know him better.

His smile warmed her through and through and helped her relax—until his attention was diverted by something he saw in the window display. His expression grew grim.

She tensed, picking up on his sudden change in mood. "What is it?"

He stepped away from her and leaned toward what looked like a battery in the window, with a large-faced gold watch attached to it.

His last words seemed to come to her through a wind tunnel. "It's a bomb. Get back."

Seconds before the blast, Joseph picked Sierra up off her feet, half dragging, half carrying her to what he hoped was safety. The explosion was like an auditory flame bursting up and crashing against his eardrums. As he made his way toward the back of the shop, a tremendous heat and wind surrounded them. He pulled Sierra to the floor as she covered her head with her arms.

The cringe and crackle of shattered glass filled the space around them right before glass showered down on them.

His arms enveloped Sierra.

It rained glass for several minutes, first a downpour and then a smattering.

Eventually quiet surrounded them. He pulled away and turned to face the gaping hole that used to be his display window. His heart was still pounding from the adrenaline rush. Though his instinct was to jump up and run to find whoever had done such a destructive thing, he turned to face Sierra. Glass glistened in her dark hair, and she had a cut above her eye. He reached out toward her.

Sierra's voice reverberated with shock. "I'm okay. I don't think anything is broken." He touched her cheek lightly and nodded. All the color had drained from her face.

The kids who had been in the alley appeared at the broken window. Much of the store inventory had been damaged by the blast and blown around. There was so much debris.

Eli, one of the older kids, shouted as he leaned through the broken window. "We called 911!"

Fearing there might be a second bomb, Joseph jumped to his feet. "Eli, you and the others stand back." Rage coursed through him. What if any kids had been in the shop at the time of the blast? They could have died. The man who accosted Sierra must have planted the bomb. And the watch on the bomb was clearly meant to let them know exactly who was responsible for the blast.

His shop had been targeted. It was another message: that they were willing to hurt people close to Sierra to get at her.

In the distance, he heard the sirens. A town the size of Scenic View would be ill-equipped to investigate what had happened here. He dared not blow his own cover by calling in DEA.

An ambulance and a police car pulled to the curb.

He turned back to face Sierra, who had gotten

to her feet but still had the look of dazed confusion on her face. She swayed. He ran over to her, placing a supportive hand around her waist.

The paramedics came through the door while a crowd began to gather. One of the police officers strung tape around the blast area while the other herded the crowd across the street.

A paramedic, a short, thin man in his early twenties, approached them. "I'm going to need to check both of you out."

"I'm fine. Why don't you deal with her first? She's got a cut on her forehead." Joseph watched the two officers working outside.

"You are still going to need to be examined," said the paramedic. "My partner, Adele, can take a look at you."

Joseph could see the other paramedic, a woman who looked to be in her forties, standing outside. The first paramedic signaled for Adele to come inside.

Joseph stepped toward the window. What he really wanted to do was figure out more about the bomb. And make sure there wasn't another bomb.

The officer stretching the crime scene tape glared at him. "Stay away from there. Let the professionals take care of that."

He took a step back. "I just want to know what happened to my shop." Would there even be an investigation? The bomb hadn't been powerful enough to destroy the whole building. But if he hadn't gotten Sierra out of the way, both of them could have been killed or maimed.

The officer glared at him. "I said step back."

Joseph looked the police officer in the eyes. "Sure, Officer. I'm just concerned there might be another bomb somewhere."

The officer eyed him, a look of suspicion crossing his features.

"Sir, I need to make sure you are okay." Adele stood beside him.

Joseph glanced at her. "I'm not hurt." A sense of urgency plagued him. All of this delay felt like such a hindrance to getting on with the investigation, to finding the man Sierra had seen in the forest.

"All the same, if you would sit down for a moment, sir." The paramedic spoke in a maternal yet scolding tone.

He rolled his eyes but complied.

While Adele checked Joseph's pupils, the male paramedic finished placing a Band-Aid on Sierra's forehead.

Adele touched Joseph's shoulder. "No signs of a head injury."

Outside, another police car pulled up. The officer approached the broken window and pulled out a tape measure.

While the paramedics packed up their medical gear, the first police officer stepped through the door. "We're going to need a statement from both of you."

Joseph scooted closer to Sierra. "Sure, Officer."

Joseph's thoughts raced at a hundred miles an hour. The shop would be closed for at least a couple of days while the cleanup and repair took place. Maybe that would give him time to get a lead on the man Sierra had seen. He could sit down with her at the computer and build a picture of the man from the program that allowed them to generate an image from facial features.

The officer turned to go, probably to get a tablet to record the statement.

Joseph came to stand beside Sierra. "After they take our statements, do you want to go up to my place and see if we can build a picture of the man you saw?"

She rubbed her eyes. "I don't want to think about this right now. I need to catch my breath."

She was clearly traumatized. Pushing her right now would not be a good idea. He had to come up with another approach. She looked up at the sky through the shattered window. "I don't even have a car. I called to have it towed. Where am I supposed to go?"

He touched her arm. "For now, you can stay with me." He laughed. "The shop is closed for the rest of the day. I need to go get my boat. You come with me, so I can keep an eye on you."

Going to get the boat would give him an opportunity to have a look around where the crime had taken place when they weren't running from a man bent on killing Sierra and taking him out as collateral damage.

Maybe going back there would help jar Sierra's memory, as well, without her feeling like there was pressure on her.

"I can call my father," said Sierra. "He can take us to your boat."

Joseph handed her his phone. As she was finishing the call, the officer came toward them holding a tablet computer.

Sierra and Joseph gave their statements to the police while they stood outside on the street. The crowd had dispersed.

Soon a man in an SUV pulled up, got out and waved at Sierra. Sierra's father was dressed in slacks and a sport jacket. His gray hair was trimmed close to his head, and his skin was lightly tanned. He had the demeanor of a stockbroker or businessman.

Sierra approached her father, who embraced her. "It sounds like you've been through a lot today, Muffin. Are you sure you don't want to come back to the house and stay the night?"

Sierra pulled free of the hug. "That's okay,

Daddy. We have things to do." A chill permeated her voice. "I don't need to go to the house. I'll be okay."

Her father glanced in the direction where the bomb had destroyed the storefront. His forehead wrinkled. "Are you sure?"

"Yes, I'm sure." Her words had an abrasive edge to them.

Sierra's dad let out a heavy sigh.

She turned to face Joseph. "This is my friend. Joseph, this is my father, Oliver Monforton."

Sierra's dad squeezed Joseph's hand with a firm, confident shake. Joseph wondered what the uncomfortable moment between father and daughter was all about.

"I heard the skateboard shop had a new manager," said Oliver.

Sierra walked toward the car, talking over her shoulder. "You can have the front seat, Joseph."

They drove out to the lakefront and along the country road, making small talk about upcoming events in Scenic View and business at the skateboard shop. Oliver dropped the two of them off not far from where the boat was stuck in the reeds. Before they took off, he offered his daughter a warm hug. "Take care, Sierra."

"I will, Daddy." Her voice was tinged with sadness.

Joseph shook Oliver's hand and thanked him

for the ride. They heard the car pull away as they made their way through the forest and brush down to the lakeshore. The boat was where they'd left it. The would-be assassin's boat was gone.

The sun rested just above the water. "We'll have to get in the water and push it out of the reeds."

"I'm down for that," said Sierra.

Though it was a warm evening, the water was cool around his legs. Sierra pulled on the bow of the boat while he pushed from behind. The water was up to his waist. The boat glided out into the deeper water. He pulled himself up. After Sierra worked her way around to the side of the boat, he reached a hand down and pulled her in.

The water dripping off their clothes sounded like a rain shower as the evening sun warmed them.

He yanked on the starter rope, and the motor sputtered to life. "I want to check out that boat and the area around it. You can show me where you saw the man with the satchel, if you're up to it."

Sierra wrapped her arms around her body. "I can handle that."

Maybe they would find some evidence. After that, he wasn't sure what his next move was.

His shop had been targeted. Going back to his apartment seemed like walking into the lion's den, and he for sure couldn't leave Sierra alone at her place. "Do you want to tell me why you didn't want to stay with your father?" At least with that arrangement, he would have some assurance of her safety. "Things seemed a little tense between the two of you."

The boat sped along through the water. Sierra sat toward the bow of the boat, watching the passing landscape. After a long moment, she turned to face him.

"When I was a teenager, my father had an affair with a much younger woman. He's married to her now. I love my father, but it's painful to return to the house I grew up in and see her there and not my mom. She was not kind to me. She saw me as a threat."

"I'm sorry. That sounds like it must have been hard."

"I don't know if my mom started taking pills and that's why Dad left her, or if she took the pills because he cheated. Everything from that time is kind of foggy. A boy I was involved with offered me stuff that took away my pain—alcohol and then some harder stuff."

"I never would have guessed that about you," he said. He felt an even deeper kinship with her. That she had been so vulnerable and that both their lives were affected by the destructive path of drugs.

"I know, I just seem so squeaky clean, like I come from a perfect family, right?"

"No, you seem so in love with God. So wanting to do the right thing by those kids."

She looked out across the water. "Been there, done that, they don't make a T-shirt for it. Anyway, that's my story." Her cheeks flushed, and she stared at the bottom of the boat.

He had picked up on the hesitation in her voice as she shared her past. It had not been easy for her to tell him the details. "It's a good story, Sierra."

She lifted her chin and smiled at him, her eyes filled with warmth. "Thank you. Maybe you can share more of your story sometime. Or does it all have to be a big secret because of your work?"

A momentary panic came over him. She was wanting to get to know him better. He could feel his defenses going up. Partly because sharing personal details in his line of work was a bad idea. More so because talking about Ezra would open up a wound he didn't care to revisit. He changed the subject.

"What happened to your mom?"

"She took too many pills one night, whether by accident or on purpose, I don't know."

He allowed the silence to settle around them. The motor hummed and water lapped against the sides of the boat with a steady rhythm.

"My crazy mixed-up family," she said. She crossed her arms over her chest. "Far from the ideal, I know."

He thought silence to be the better answer to all that she had told him.

Sierra's was a life marked by immense pain. Yet she chose to love God and to care and to risk herself where the kids were concerned.

They skirted around some rocks jutting out of the water and rounded a cove. The dilapidated boat came into view. He steered toward the shore, stopping when the water grew shallow. He killed the motor, and they both got out to pull the boat up to the beach.

Sierra stood staring at the wrecked boat and the forest beyond. He wrapped an arm around her back and drew her close. He knew from experience that going back to the place where a victim had experienced or even witnessed violence could be helpful, but could also bring back some of the terror Sierra had been through. "I'm right here with you, Sierra. Let me have a look around the boat, and then you can take me to where you saw the man."

Joseph reached out for the broken rope ladder and started to climb.

When he was almost to the top, Sierra's frantic voice reached his ears. "Someone's in the bushes."

SIX

Fear made Sierra's muscles turn to stone. Her heart raged against her rib cage and her pulse drummed in her ears. While a voice inside her head screamed *go, go!*, she remained paralyzed.

Joseph leaped down from the boat, his feet hitting the sand with a thud.

She caught a flash of blond hair and denim in the greenery. A girl dashed from the tangle of brush. She peered back over her shoulder and then ran faster. The girl kept running, not even noticing Sierra.

Daisy. Trevor's little sister. No longer frozen by fear, Sierra took off after Daisy. She pushed the low-hanging branches out of the way. She caught flashes of color and heard the girl's footfalls. Daisy was headed up toward the road.

Sierra arrived on the road just in time to see Daisy getting on a bike. She wore a small pack. The teenager pedaled away, gaining speed.

Sierra ran after her. "Stop! I need to talk to

you about Trevor!" But she was so out of breath, her voice didn't carry.

The girl pedaled faster. Sierra sprinted, leaning into the wind. Daisy swooped down a hill, gaining speed. Unable to run any farther, Sierra stopped and watched the bike disappear around a bend.

Joseph came up behind her. "What's going on?"

Sierra sucked in a breath. "That girl was Trevor's little sister. Something had her really scared. I'm not sure if she even heard me."

Joseph put his hands on his hips. "All of this connects somehow."

"We need to get back into town so I can talk to Daisy. Maybe she wasn't being honest when I talked to her earlier. She might know something about Trevor."

He tugged on her shirt. "Let's search the boat." He hurried back through the forest. "Maybe we can figure out why she would pedal her bike all the way out here."

Sierra followed behind. She stepped into the clearing where she had seen the man with the satchel. A chill ran over her skin. "This is the place."

Joseph turned to face her.

She closed her eyes. When she tried to remember the man's face, the picture in her mind was blurred. "What I remember most is how he was dressed. His clothes looked like he'd just bought them. Crisp jacket, a polo shirt and slacks, not what you wear when you are going to be hiking in a forest or walking on the beach."

Joseph shifted his weight from one foot to the other. He tilted his head. "Interesting. Maybe he wasn't supposed to be out here. Maybe his delivery guy flaked on him. The higher-ups usually try to keep their hands clean."

She was still upset about seeing Daisy out here.

"While we're here, let's search that boat and get back to town as fast as we can," Joseph said.

"Yes, I want to talk to Daisy. It will take her longer to get back into town on that bike. Can I borrow your phone to text her foster mom? She might be able to go out and pick Daisy up on the road." She sent the text and handed the phone back to him.

Joseph waited until she stepped toward him to push his way through the brush. They walked beside each other down to the shore. "I'll boost you up on deck. I'll keep watch while you look around."

She caught his gaze for a moment. Her heart beat a little faster. Clearly, this place was a hot spot for activity. He wasn't taking any chances.

He laced his fingers together to serve as a

stirrup for her to put her foot in. She gripped the broken ladder. "I'll push you up so you can grab the edge of the deck."

"Okay." Her muscles strained as she gripped the abrasive rope. She remembered how easily Joseph had scaled the broken ladder without any help. He was in way better shape than she was.

He pushed from below, and she reached up for the edge of the boat. She pulled herself up and stared at the deck. The boat creaked as she walked around. She picked up some dirty fabric that may have been part of a sail, and kicked some boards out of the way. She walked to the edge of the boat, while Joseph paced with his hand inside his coat where his gun was.

"It all looks the same up here. I'm going below deck."

Joseph planted his feet and continued to survey the forest. "I don't think that's a good idea. Not alone. What if someone is below deck? I'll come up there with you."

His hypervigilance made her nervous. Seeing Daisy so scared bothered her, too. What or who had frightened the girl? They needed to hurry and get out of here.

Joseph's voice floated up to her. "Sierra, I think I see something." He walked away from the boat toward the bushes.

Her heart skipped a beat as she headed toward the rope.

It took her a minute to jump to the ground. Joseph was standing just outside some brush along the shoreline holding something.

"I found this over farther down the shore. The color caught my eye." He held up a lime-green backpack. "Someone built a fire on the shore. Not too long ago. The coals were still warm."

Sierra took the backpack. There were cartoons on the front pocket. Something a preschooler would be attracted to. The canvas backpack was frayed, and the material was dirty. "I've never seen it before." She unzipped the larger pocket and pulled out an empty candy wrapper. Her hand touched fabric, and she pulled out Trevor's red windbreaker. "It's Trevor's."

"Check the pockets."

The first pocket was empty. She unzipped the second pocket, which contained a compact Bible. "This gives me hope that Trevor is trying to get back to God."

"He's clearly in some kind of struggle between two worlds," Joseph said. "I know what that battle is like." His voice faltered.

She gazed at him for a moment. He seemed to be speaking from a deeply emotional place. Joseph was such a solid person. She'd pictured him coming from a stable family. Not messed up like hers. Maybe in his line of work, he'd seen addiction take people to places they never intended to go. The emotion in his voice suggested the experience was a little closer to home.

"Daisy had a pack on her back. Maybe she was bringing food or other supplies for her brother. The two siblings are very close and loyal to each other. Trevor might have been hiding out or waiting."

He didn't answer right away. "Maybe. The dealers probably moved their operation away from here, knowing they'd been spotted. Maybe Trevor thought it would be safe."

And maybe he was pulling Daisy into the darkness, too. The thought sent a whole new wave of fear crashing through her. "This area is a familiar hideout for kids." Whatever Trevor was into, she just couldn't picture him putting his sister in harm's way.

Joseph lifted his head. "Someone is moving through the trees."

The distinct crack of a branch breaking reached her ears.

He tugged on her shirtsleeve as her heart revved into overdrive. "We better get out of here," he said.

* * *

"What if it's Trevor coming back?" Her eyes were pleading.

"We don't know whose side he's on." He had to admire her for caring about Trevor, but none of this looked good for the kid.

There was no time to argue. He grabbed Sierra's hand and dragged her back toward the shore. Two men emerged through the trees before they could hide. One was Baseball Hat man. The other was built like a brick house, muscular and broad through the shoulders. A look of surprise crossed the men's faces when they saw Sierra and Joseph. Baseball Hat reached for his gun.

Joseph and Sierra ran along the rocky shore toward the boat. Sierra stumbled and fell. He stopped to help her to her feet as the men closed in on them. One of them fired a shot. Their boat was within twenty yards.

The rocky shore changed to sand, and they ran toward the boat. They both jumped in the water and pushed the boat toward deeper water. Sierra jumped in while Joseph pulled the starter rope.

Baseball Hat ran toward them while the bulkier man slowed. He seemed to have lost his wind. Sierra crouched down low in the boat. "That's the man who came into the shop."

Joseph steered the motorboat into deep water.

Another shot zinged through the air. He gave a backward glance to the men on the shore as they grew smaller and farther away. Hopefully, the men had come by car and would not be able to chase them.

Fishermen's Crest was a hot spot for the drug trade. He would inform DEA, and they might set up surveillance. That was something he could not be a part of because it would risk blowing his cover. The surveillance might be in vain; after so much activity, a smart distributor might get paranoid and move his operation. And yet, those two men had shown up here. Had they come out here looking for Trevor? Maybe Daisy had seen the men and become frightened.

Sierra sat up in the boat, glancing over her shoulder. "I think we lost them."

The sun was low on the horizon as he steered the boat back to civilization. Minutes passed without either of them talking. The water took on a warm appearance as the sky around them turned pink and orange.

He glanced over at Sierra, who brushed a strand of dark hair off her face. The evening light made her skin glow. She had shared so much about the heartache in her own life. He found himself wanting to open up to her, wanting to be closer to her, but knowing it was a bad idea.

Protection for her wouldn't be set up for a couple of days. Even then, he worried whether it would be enough. With the shop closed until the window could be replaced and the explosive damage cleaned up, she wouldn't be able to stay close under the guise of doing his books.

Up ahead, he saw the twinkling lights of Stardust Cove, a cluster of shops and restaurants that was reachable only by boat. "Are you hungry?"

She touched her stomach. "Starving. If Daisy is biking in from Fisherman's Crest, we probably have time to grab a bite before she gets back into town."

The truth was, after they talked to Daisy, he wasn't sure what to do. He couldn't just drop Sierra off at her place, and he didn't think going back to his would be safe, either. The chattering harmonies of people eating, visiting and having a good time reached his ears as he docked the boat.

He tied it off and reached his hand out to help Sierra. People were dressed in sundresses and swimsuits. Their damp clothes did not look totally out of place. As they sat at the outdoor café, still on high alert, Joseph picked a table in the corner so his back would be to the wall and he could watch people coming and going.

Sierra scooted her seat close to the bistro table as a waitress brought them menus.

The waitress, who looked to be barely out of her teens, planted her feet. Recognition spread across Sierra's face. She jumped to her feet and hugged the waitress. "Jamie, it's so good to see you." She turned to face Joseph. "Jamie is one of the alums from youth group."

"Good to see you, Miss Monforton." Jamie shifted her gaze to Joseph. "And out on a date."

Color rose up in Sierra's cheeks. "Oh no, it's nothing like that. We're just a—" She looked to Joseph for an explanation.

Joseph shrugged, not sure what to say but amused by Sierra's embarrassment.

Jamie smiled. "Well, all I can say is it's about time." She winked at Sierra. "The soup of the day is clam chowder. We're all out of the coconut shrimp." Jamie floated over to another table to ask the people how their meal was.

He scanned the menu. "The soup sounds good."

Still blushing, Sierra sat back down and stared at the menu. "I might get a grilled cheese with it. Comfort food on a cool summer night."

He studied her as she flipped through the menu.

Another problem niggled at the corner of his mind. The closer he stayed to Sierra, the greater the risk of his cover being blown. Why would a skateboard shop manager suddenly become a bodyguard to a woman whose life was under threat?

"It wouldn't be a bad thing, you know."

She looked up, blue eyes shining. "What?"

"If we were a couple...as part of my cover."

Her mouth formed a perfect O but she didn't respond.

"People are going to start to wonder why we're always together." He leaned over the table and spoke in a lower voice. "I can't risk my cover being blown."

She studied him for a long moment. "I understand. For pretend."

He nodded. He wouldn't be pretending that much. Though he knew nothing could come of it, he liked Sierra, admired her, even. But he was here to do a job, and he couldn't let this go beyond a friendship.

Jamie came back and took their order, still grinning at Sierra and shaking her head. Once Jamie had stepped away, Sierra leaned closer to Joseph. "I'm sure Jamie will get the buzz going about the two of us being an item. By tomorrow, the whole of Scenic View will know."

He nodded. "It's a plan, then." He stared out at the water, enjoying this calm, this brief oasis. He could get used to this, just being with Sierra. He dismissed the thought as quickly as it had come into his head.

He pushed the phone toward her. "See if the foster mom answered the text."

"It's still too soon for Daisy to have biked all the way back." She picked up the phone and clicked through. "Margaret says she couldn't find Daisy on the road she should have been on when she searched it by car. She called the police. They're searching for Daisy, as well." Her voice filled with concern. "I just can't see Trevor involving his little sister in all this. He's always been so protective of her."

A different waitress brought them their food.

He wanted to reassure her, but at the same time she needed to be realistic. His experience told him that people did all kinds of things they normally wouldn't do if drugs had a hold of their soul. "I think it's really great how much you clearly care about these kids."

"Thank you." Her voice took on a warm quality, and when she looked at him with those blue eyes, he felt an urge to lean in closer to her.

He broke off the intensity of the moment by scooping up a spoonful of the clam chowder. "This looks good." He enjoyed the creamy saltiness of the soup. Sierra picked up her sandwich. Cheese dripped out of the bottom as she took a bite.

"That looks really gooey."

She licked her lips. "It's quite wonderful, actually. Do you want a bite?"

He wasn't sure what to say to that.

She tilted her head toward another table, where Jamie was sneaking glimpses of them while she talked with a group of teenagers. "Just to continue the fiction that we're a couple." She handed him the other half of the sandwich.

"Oh, right." He took a bite and handed it back to her. "Mmm. That is good comfort food."

They finished their meal and returned to the boat. The lake was less crowded this time of night. A large commercial boat went by, filled with partygoers standing on the lighted deck, laughing and talking.

Joseph guided the boat into a narrower gap in the lake where they were the only boat. Sierra sat in the seat beside him.

He raised his voice above the chugging of the motor. "I rent a dock just up here a ways."

She nodded. "Maybe Daisy showed up at her home by now."

The lighted dock came into view. There were three other boats already docked and two docks that were still empty. Joseph steered the boat toward one of the empty docks. The boat swayed as he stepped out onto the pier to tie it off.

He held his hand out for Sierra as she lifted her foot to step from the boat to the solid wooden pier. Her hand felt silky smooth in his when he pulled her up. They stood facing each other for a moment. A surge of electricity passed through him when she made eye contact.

Then she turned away, wrapping her arms around herself. She tilted her head toward the starry sky. "It's a beautiful night."

"Yes, it is. There is a taxi service I can call to come get us and bring us back into town." He touched her arm lightly. He wondered if she had experienced the same feeling of attraction in that moment.

"Where are we going?" Her voice filled with affection that made his heart beat faster. She glanced at him and then looked away.

The moment had become uncomfortable. What did it matter if he was starting to have feelings for her? He was in Scenic View to do a job. "Like you said, maybe Daisy will have shown up by then."

He got out his phone and held it toward the light. Something pinged against it, and it flew out of his hand.

It wasn't until the second shot that it registered in his head that they were being hunted again. Sierra had hit the ground after the first bullet had shattered his phone.

The second must have been aimed at her, though it had gone wild.

Sierra jumped up and raced toward the shelter of the trees. He sprinted after her as fear and excitement raged through him.

He'd let his guard down. Of course, the hired muscle had been sent to watch the dock, and he'd been there, waiting for their return.

SEVEN

The forest fell silent around Sierra. The only sound she heard was her own breathing and the padding of her footsteps. The thickness of the trees slowed her progress. Where had the shooter gone?

She stopped to look around and listen.

Joseph came up behind her. His sprint had turned into a jog. He glanced from side to side and then stood beside her.

The stillness was eerie.

He leaned close and whispered in her ear. "It's a long trek back to town. I say we get back to the boat."

As he spoke, his breath warmed the side of her face. Before they were plunged back into the nightmare of being stalked, a moment had passed between them on the dock. She'd felt the surge of attraction as they stood facing each other.

All of that had been washed away with the gunfire.

"Don't you think they'll be watching the dock?"

He leaned close to her, their shoulders touching. He didn't respond right away. He turned his head, still listening. "We'd be too much of a target trying to walk back into town."

If the shooter wasn't coming after them, he must be watching the dock.

She heard a rustling of tree branches. Could be a bird…or a man.

Heart pounding, she edged toward the trunk of a large cottonwood. Joseph pressed against a tree, as well.

He was right about the long walk into town. There was the possibility that there were two men waiting to take them out. It had happened before. One to follow them through the forest and the other to watch the dock.

"What if we swam back to the boat?" she said. "That would be unexpected."

Joseph nodded.

A sound that could have been footsteps reached her ears as she peeled herself off the tree trunk and took a step toward the water's edge. Both of them tiptoed. Though they moved at a snail's pace to make as little noise as possible, her heart pounded out an erratic beat that pulsed in her ears and seemed to fill the forest.

Water lapped against the shore as the trees grew farther apart. At this part of the lake, there was no beach. The trees jutted up against an abrupt drop-off.

As she slipped into the water, she heard a distinctly human sound in the forest and saw a flash of light. She slipped underneath the water just as light reached the edge of the water.

She swam underwater until she could hold her breath no longer, then bobbed to the surface. She didn't see Joseph anywhere. Light flashed along the shore. She slipped back under the water as the illumination touched the surface of the lake above her.

Careful not to stir the surface of the water, she kicked in the general direction of the dock, trusting that Joseph was headed in the same direction. The water enveloped her and pressed on her eardrums, making her feel insulated from the violence that probably awaited her on the shore.

When she broke through to the surface of the water, the lights of the dock shimmered in the darkness. She dove under and swam until she could touch the legs of the pier that were underwater. She slipped under the pier with her head above water.

Still no sign of Joseph. She could reach the boat with her hand as it bobbed and swayed.

She swam out to the far side of the boat and lifted her head just above the rim. Though it was summer, the cold water and the evening chill soaked through her skin. She saw no signs of activity on the shore. The flashlight of the man who had taken a shot at her earlier winked in and out of view as the man searched the trees and shoreline.

She studied each tree and each shadow, looking for movement or anything that might be a second human being lying in wait. Still seeing nothing, she slipped back underneath the pier.

The tricky part would be untying the boat. She'd be easy enough to spot once she was on the pier.

Down the shoreline, the light from the first shooter drew closer.

It would be a matter of minutes before he was back at the dock. She gripped the edge of the pier and then pulled herself up. Water swooshed around her and dribbled off her clothes. The noise was distinct from the other sounds around her.

She hurried over to where the boat was tied off, glancing from side to side and then toward the water. What on earth had happened to Joseph?

A gunshot resounded from the trees down-shore. The first shooter had spotted her.

Up shore, a shadowy figure moved toward her. It took her a moment to recognize Joseph's silhouette. Another figure jumped out of the trees and leaped at Joseph, taking him to the ground. The sound of flesh smashing into flesh greeted her as the two men fought.

She jumped in the boat, turned the key in the ignition, steered out of the dock and headed toward where Joseph still wrestled with the other man.

Joseph was on top of him. He landed a blow to the guy's face that left him motionless.

She angled the boat so the headlight shone where Joseph and the man fought.

"He's out cold," said Joseph as he rose to his feet. He leaned a little closer to the man he had been fighting with. "He's just a kid." His voice filled with anguish.

Downshore, the first shooter was getting into one of the other boats, preparing to chase them.

Joseph ran into the water and swam toward the boat.

Shock spread through Sierra while she waited for Joseph to get to the boat. The kid lying on the shore out cold, the one who had attacked Joseph, was Trevor.

* * *

Sierra kept glancing over at the kid who had attacked Joseph as she reached a hand out for him to get in the boat.

"It's Trevor." Her voice sounded far away and filled with pain. "He's the one who attacked you."

Joseph barely had time to register what she had said as another, bigger boat barreled toward them. He hurried to start the engine and steer it out into open water.

It was clear now whose side Trevor was on. The reality probably hit Sierra like a blow to the stomach.

There was no time to process it or offer support. The roar of the other boat overtook them. The boat the shooter had taken was twice the size of his. He couldn't hope to outrun the guy, but his boat was more nimble. He might be able to outmaneuver him if he could get a little distance between him.

He pulled his gun from the holster. "Can you shoot?"

"A little."

He handed her the gun. She inched closer to him, crouched low and steadied it by resting her hands on the edge of the boat. She got off one shot. The other boat slowed momentarily.

Joseph turned the wheel so quickly that Sierra slammed against him.

"I dropped the gun."

He could hear it sliding around the floor of the boat.

Joseph stared ahead, trying to remember the layout of this part of the lake. "Don't worry about it."

Several lakefront houses whizzed by in his peripheral vision, all of them dark or with only a single outdoor light on. The lake widened.

He glanced over his shoulder. The other boat was several yards behind them.

Joseph pressed the throttle all the way down. He entered a part of the lake that was so wide, he could see only one shoreline. The other side was vast open water. This was his chance to outmaneuver the other boat.

His boat angled to one side, spraying water on them as Joseph flipped it around and sped past the other boat. Knowing that it would take longer for the bigger boat to turn in the water, he felt that might give him the advantage he needed.

Sierra craned her neck. "He's still turning."

"Good, let me know when and if he slips out of sight."

The lake turned in a serpentine pattern and

then narrowed again. The boat skimmed the waves as though it were a solid surface.

"I can't see him anymore." Sierra turned around to face forward.

The trees grew close to the shore and hung over the water. Joseph slipped into a cove behind a snag of fallen logs and debris. The overhanging trees provided them with additional cover. Joseph killed the engine and turned off the lights just as the other boat sped by.

They sat in the stillness and the dark for a long moment as his boat bobbed on the water.

"Do you think he saw us and is just turning around?"

Joseph didn't reply right away. Instead he listened for the sound of another boat.

Only the lapping of the water reached his ears. "This is our chance to get out of here." He clicked the lights on and turned the key in the ignition.

He maneuvered the boat out into the center of the lake and turned around, headed in the opposite direction the other boat had gone. Several houses appeared on the shore, and in the distance the glittering lights of the resort came into view.

"I'm sorry about Trevor," he said.

"It breaks my heart," she said. "I just hope he hasn't drawn his little sister into all the trouble."

"It's late, but I still think we should find out if she made it home and go talk to her. I'll dock by the resort."

Joseph sped through the open water. Only one other boat passed by them. Sierra glanced nervously behind her.

He tensed as he studied the water in front of him. "All clear?"

"So far." She turned around and sat down beside him.

Up ahead, he saw lights from several other boats. Traffic increased as they got close to the resort. He brought the boat into dock and they stepped out on the boardwalk. The resort was a ten-story hotel, with shops and restaurants on the bottom floor.

"I know it's late, but we need to find or borrow a phone to call and let the foster mom know we're coming over to talk to Daisy...if she's back," he said.

They stepped inside the resort. It was warm inside. Most the shops were closed, but they found a restaurant that was open and had only a few customers. The manager let them use the reservation phone.

Sierra pressed in the number and waited. "Hello, Margaret, this is Sierra. I know it's late, but is Daisy home yet?" Her voice had a hopeful lilt.

Joseph's chest felt as though it was in a vise being twisted tighter and tighter.

An older couple walked by them, chatting. Sierra stepped away so she could hear Margaret. There was a long pause and then her shoulders slumped. "Oh, I see…and the police haven't found her?"

So something had happened to Daisy, too.

After hanging up the phone, she turned to face him. "She never came home." She shook her head in disbelief as her eyes glazed with tears. "I just can't believe Trevor would pull his sister into all this. She mattered more to him than anyone in the world."

"When drugs become your God, nothing else matters."

"How would you know?" Her voice broke and she walked away from him swiping at her eyes.

He hurried after her. The walkway and seating areas outside the shops had marble floors that glistened in the warm lights that hung from the ceiling. Above him, people sat on the balconies of their hotel rooms and gazed down to the resort floor. A trickle of people moved in and out of the bars and restaurants, many of them dressed in swimwear and cover-ups.

He had a moment of panic when he glanced

around, looking for Sierra, and didn't see her. From the beginning of all this, he had the feeling that the forces they were dealing with might have eyes and ears everywhere. Was it possible she'd been kidnapped? He quickened his pace around a corner that led to a corridor of smaller shops.

Sierra sat on a lush couch, staring out a window that looked onto the water. Still not noticing him, she rose to her feet, crossed her arms and stepped closer to the floor-to-ceiling window.

The tension left his body. "Sierra."

She looked over at him, her features twisted with sadness.

He rushed toward her and gathered her into his arms. The thought of her being in danger, of losing her, had been like a blow to the stomach for him. Maybe it was all that they had been through together, but he felt closer to her than he'd felt with any woman since he'd chosen undercover work. He'd always thought his work would be enough, but now he wasn't so sure. There was something nourishing and safe about being close to Sierra.

He held her for a long moment, drawing her close. She pressed her face against his chest, crying softly.

His throat went tight. "I do know what it's

like, Sierra…to lose someone." Warmth pooled in the corners of his eyes.

She pulled back and gazed at him.

He felt as though he were pulling the words up from the bottoms of his feet. "My brother… he was only seventeen."

Her expression softened as she raised her hand and touched his cheek. "I had no idea."

His heart opened up to her even more as her tenderness drew him in. Sharing with her made the load he carried seem lighter.

So few people knew of the pain that drove him to do such dangerous work. None of it would ever bring Ezra back, but maybe he could keep another kid from the brink. Tonight, though, was washed in defeat because of the revelation about Trevor.

An older woman dressed in an evening gown walked by and stopped to stare at them. Heat rose up in his cheeks and he pulled away, swiping at his own eyes. Sierra laid a supportive hand on his upper back. Her featherlight touch warmed him to his core.

The old woman tilted her chin, lifted the skirt of her gown and walked away.

He turned around to face Sierra. He could drown in the warm pool of her eyes. She offered him a faint smile. "Margaret said that she called the police and filed a missing persons report for Daisy. She already filed one for Trevor. He hasn't been home since the night I was supposed to meet him out at Fisherman's Crest." Her voice faltered.

He touched her arm just above the elbow. "We might still be able to save Daisy if we can figure out what has happened to her. You said they were close. Maybe she's trying to help Trevor."

"I'm not sure where to start. I feel like we need to hit all the places the kids hang out—the skateboard park, the ice cream shop. Somebody might know something. I can call all the kids from youth group. They talk to each other. They text." Sierra's voice grew more and more frantic as she spoke.

He grabbed her hands. "Tomorrow, Sierra. We need to get some sleep. We both do."

"But I'm worried about Daisy. If the police are involved with the drug trade, are they even going to be out looking for her?"

"Not all of them are involved. Would you do me a favor? Would you consider staying at your father's tonight, so I know you're safe?"

She nodded. "Yes, I can stand one night of my stepmother's coldness. I wouldn't be able to sleep at my place alone, anyway."

"I need to make some calls in the morning. To get the ball rolling on getting the shop window replaced," he said. "I have to look like I'm running a business."

"I understand. I'll make calls in the morning, too, figure out a strategy for finding Daisy," she said.

They phoned a taxi and waited outside the resort. The night sky twinkled with stars. The taxi pulled to the curb, and they both slipped into the back seat. Sierra gave the driver directions.

As they sat together, he felt closer to her than he had felt to a woman in a long time. Once he'd chosen undercover work, he had pretty much been married to his job. But being around Sierra unlocked something inside him.

The taxi reached the edge of town and then turned up a long, winding paved road. They passed no other houses on the way to Sierra's father's house.

The taxi pulled up to large wrought iron gates.

"I need to punch the code in." She jumped out of the taxi and walked over to a box positioned by the gates. They eased open and she reentered the taxi. It rolled along on a driveway made of large flat stones. Trees obscured the house until they were right in front of it.

The brick house towered three stories above him with a large, sweeping stairway spanning the whole front of the house. It reminded Joseph of the courthouse in the small Georgia town he'd grown up in.

His mouth went dry. "What did you say your father does for a living?"

She hung her head slightly and whispered, "He's a finance guy."

She pushed open the door and hurried up the stairs with a backward glance and a wave before pressing in another code and disappearing behind the wooden double doors.

Joseph sat back in his seat. "Well, Jeeves, onward to my humble abode."

The taxi driver whistled. "Some people and their money, huh?"

"Indeed."

As the taxi wound down the road and back into town, whatever closeness he'd felt to Sierra seemed to fade. He thought of the trailer house he'd grown up in. The car on blocks in the backyard and his father's hunting hounds baying in their kennel.

Scenic View was not his world. And he did not belong in Sierra's. Whatever closeness he felt with her, he had to let it go.

The taxi drove through downtown Scenic View and stopped in front of the skateboard shop, where boards had been placed over the display window and a sign that read Closed for Repairs hung on the door.

He made his way up the back stairs to his apartment with a heavy heart.

The number one rule of undercover work was not to form attachments. He'd be on to another assignment sooner or later. Whatever he was beginning to feel for Sierra, he knew he couldn't let it develop into anything more.

He unlocked his door and stepped inside the silent, dark space of his apartment.

EIGHT

Sierra woke early, hoping to leave her father's house before encountering her stepmother. Allison was only eight years older than Sierra. Though most of the tension between them was caused by Allison seeing Sierra as some sort of threat and resenting any time her father spent with her, Sierra knew that she bore some ill feelings toward Allison because she was a reminder of how their once happy family had fallen apart.

She'd had only brief words with her father when she'd come in. As late as it had been, he was in his study still working on his laptop— some sort of international business that required he be up at such a late hour.

She and her father had lunch together at least once a week, and she loved being out on his boat when it was just the two of them. But something about their relationship remained fractured.

She crept down the stairs, past the kitchen,

where Allison was standing by the window with her cup of coffee. "Oliver said you had spent the night." Her voice had a hard edge to it.

"I'll call a taxi and be out of your hair in no time."

"Oliver said you could take one of the cars. I guess yours is out of commission." She took a sip of her coffee.

The hostility between the two of them had changed to a cordial coolness. Sierra was no longer an angry, confused, drug-using teenager. Though the pain was still there, her prayer was always that she would walk in forgiveness toward Allison and her father. "Thank you, Allison. I appreciate it."

She hurried down the back stairs and across the walkway that led to the garage. Her father owned five cars.

She grabbed the keys for the SUV, clicked open the garage door and headed for home. Once there, she showered and was preparing to make a cup of coffee when her landline rang.

It wasn't a number she recognized.

"Miss M." Trevor's voice sounded desperate and filled with anguish as soon as she answered. "You have to help."

"Trevor. I know this is a setup. I saw you attack—" She took in a breath. "I saw you attack my boyfriend. And you set us up when we went out to the junkyard."

"It's not like that."

As always, his voice sounded so sincere. "Okay, meet me in a public place, then."

"I can't. I can't be seen in town. I'm in danger."

"Where's Daisy? What has happened to her?"

"She's safe for now. Miss M, we really need your help."

"Trevor, you have to tell me what is going on. What have you dragged Daisy into?"

"There's no time. I'm at that cabin. The writer's cabin. I don't know how long it will be safe to stay here. They always find me. Wherever I go, they find me."

The line went dead.

Sierra stared at the phone while her heart thudded. She closed her eyes and prayed for guidance. The story of the lost sheep came to mind. God values every life no matter what that person has done. At the same time, she needed to think of her own safety…and Daisy's. Daisy was probably at the cabin, too. There was still a chance to save her.

She dialed Joseph's landline number. He picked up on the first ring.

"It's Trevor. He's says he's at my friend's

cabin and he's in danger. Daisy is probably there with him."

"You know this is a setup, right? Just like before."

"I accept that Trevor is lost to that life, but what about Daisy?" Her throat went tight, and she could feel the tears about to come. "What if we still have a shot at helping Daisy? She's only thirteen years old. Regardless of what he has done, I can't imagine him putting his sister in harm's way or wanting to draw her into the drug life."

There was a long pause on the other end of the line.

"I can't do this alone, Joseph. It's too dangerous and I don't have the training."

Again, more silence.

She closed her eyes and prayed. At the end of the day, she wanted to be able to say she'd done everything she could for each of these kids.

"He probably has information that would be helpful to the investigation." Joseph cleared his throat. "Swing around and pick me up at the back of the shop."

She let out the breath she'd been holding. "I'm on my way."

Joseph was waiting in the alley when she pulled up. He jumped into the passenger seat.

The bulge on his side told her that he had his gun with him.

She sped out of town along a road that bordered the lake before turning onto a one-lane road that led up a mountain.

Joseph hadn't said anything since getting into the car.

"The lake curves around. We came into the cabin from the other side when we went there."

"We need to approach with extreme caution. Pull off the road before we get to the cabin." His voice was businesslike and a little cold.

"Thank you for helping me."

"Wish I had some backup. There was no time to put it in place. Some more DEA guys are headed in to do surveillance at Fisherman's Crest. I told Jake, my clerk, that I was going to help a drugged-out kid and that it might get dangerous. We may have to call the sheriff. He's county, not city."

It felt as though a weight pressed on her chest. "I hope it's just a fifteen-year-old kid and his sister."

"Me, too," Joseph said. "At the very least, if we can take Trevor in, he might be able to answer some questions."

She drove on for some time in silence. They were both motivated by the same thing—saving young lives. She only hoped it wasn't a fool's errand. "There is a place up ahead where the car can't be seen from the road, so there's no chance it will be tampered with again."

She pulled into the grove of trees. Early morning sun warmed her skin as she got out of the car and closed the door softly. Joseph had already pulled his weapon and was surveying the forest and the road beyond.

She stood close to him and whispered, "We're about a hundred yards from the cabin. We can cut through the trees and not be seen if anyone is watching the place."

Joseph took the lead, moving quickly but quietly through the evergreens. The cabin came into view. Joseph crouched in the trees, watching, waiting.

The place seemed quiet. No sign of movement through the windows.

Joseph ran forward and crouched. She scooted in behind him. He leaned close and whispered, "I'll go in. You wait here. I'll give you the all-clear by standing by that window." He handed her his phone. He must have gotten another one. "If anything happens to me, call the sheriff's office, not the city police."

She nodded. She knew he was trying to protect her from what might be an ambush. She gripped the branch of the tree and prayed for Joseph's safety.

With his weapon drawn, Joseph eased the door open and disappeared inside. The cabin had been unlocked. Trevor would have known where the key was. Joseph flashed past the window, headed toward the other room.

Tension corseted around her heart as the seconds ticked by. She turned her head slightly, studying the forest around her. Several trees away, five birds took off, their wings flapping. Her heart fluttered. Something had disturbed them. Animal or human, she couldn't tell.

She turned her attention back to the cabin. A stillness settled around her while she watched the window. Still no sign of Joseph.

A branch broke off to her side. Someone or something was in these woods.

Heart racing, she bolted up from her hiding place and moved toward the cover of a cluster of trees, padding lightly but quickly on the forest floor.

She stopped and crouched low. Though she was as still as a rock, her heart beat wildly.

She peered through the leaves at the cabin. Something must have happened to Joseph. She ran toward a shed and crouched beside it, surveying the area around her.

Wind rustled the leaves. Branches creaked. She stared at the phone. The sheriff wouldn't be able to get here fast enough. She phoned them anyway, letting them know what was going on without giving up Joseph's true identity.

She jumped up and sprinted the final length to the cabin. She heard the zing of a bullet just as she reached the threshold of the cabin and dropped to the floor. The sound was that of a rifle, not a pistol. The shooter could be quite far away.

She got down on all fours to move past the window. Joseph wasn't in the living room or the kitchen. Only days ago, they had sat in front of that fireplace, relishing the momentary safety of this secluded cabin.

The cabin was not that big. She checked the downstairs bedroom—empty. She climbed the ladder to the loft space with three twin mattresses. The loft had a huge window that looked out on the forest.

She stood on the third-to-last rung of the wooden ladder, her head just above the floor of the loft.

She heard footsteps on the wood floor. Someone was in the cabin.

She thought to call out Joseph's name, but decided not to. Instead, she scrambled up to the loft and hid behind a dresser. Frozen with fear, she listened to the sound of the approaching footsteps.

* * *

Joseph came to, lying flat on his back with a view of the trees above him. He touched his forehead where it hurt. When he looked at his fingers, there was blood on them. Someone had hit him, knocking him unconscious and dragged him into the trees. He sat up. His gun was gone.

This was clearly an ambush. Once again, Trevor was probably not even on the property.

He was only a short distance from the cabin. Someone had wanted him out of commission so they could get to Sierra. Or they saw their opportunity with Sierra and would get to him later. His head throbbed and his vision blurred as he pushed himself to his feet.

He needed to get to Sierra before the man who had hit him did. His mind was foggy from the blow. A man had come at him from behind a door before he could clear it.

He stumbled as he ran into the forest, past the cabin to where he'd left Sierra. His heart stopped. She wasn't there. Had she gone into the cabin looking for him? Maybe she'd just found a better hiding place...and maybe someone had found her.

Gunfire came at him from the side. He dropped to the ground and soldier-crawled toward a large rock. He watched the area where the gunfire had come from, some trees off to the side. A pistol at close range. He'd never find Sierra if he had to dodge gunfire. And a gun would ensure they could get away.

He circled around through the trees, seeking to flank the man who had fired at him. As he moved through the trees, he caught a hint of noise that was distinctly human. He did not see so much as he sensed where the other man was. His pursuer was on the move, searching for him.

He caught a flash of color—yellow. Now he knew where the guy was. He hurried from tree to tree until he could see the man's back. It was their old friend Baseball Hat. His cap was a light yellow, almost white.

Joseph dove at the man, landing a blow to his lower back where his kidney was. The man groaned in pain. He whirled around. Joseph hit the man in the face and then his head. Baseball Hat crumpled to the ground, unconscious.

Joseph grabbed the man's gun where it had fallen and stepped over the body.

Now to find Sierra and get out of here.

NINE

Sierra peered out from behind the dresser. Her heart stopped. Trevor stepped through the living room toward the loft. His hands were empty. No gun. No knife.

Just as she had done, he checked the main floor bedroom first. She slipped out from behind the dresser and waited until he walked past the loft. She fell on him, taking him to the floor. Trevor lay on his stomach. She sat with both knees on his back.

"Where's Daisy?"

"She's not here. She's safe. You have to help us get out of town."

"You set us up. Just like before."

"No." His voice filled with anguish. "Please. Let me explain."

She lessened some of the pressure on his back. His cheek was pressed against the floor as he talked.

"They told me they would hurt Daisy if I

didn't do what they said. They made me call you about coming out to the junkyard."

"Why didn't you wait for me on the road when I came to get you at Fisherman's Crest?"

"I saw those men and I got scared. Please, Miss M. You've got to believe me." Trevor started to cry.

She let up a little more pressure. They didn't have a lot of time. There was at least one man with a rifle outside, probably more.

Trevor continued to sob. "I never wanted to hurt you or Daisy."

"How did those men get up here, then?"

"They must have followed you. I hiked up here at night. They know I hid Daisy. If they find us, they will kill us." Desperation colored every word he uttered. "They caught Daisy when she was leaving Fisherman's Crest. They said if I didn't hurt your boyfriend out there on the dock, they would hurt her."

His story seemed really discombobulated, but his remorse seemed real. "But you said she was safe?"

"She got away and then I found a hiding place for her, but we need to get out of town."

Trevor had a lot of explaining to do, but now was not the time. For Daisy's sake, she would get him out of here. She slipped off his back and pushed herself to her feet. "We don't have much time. We have to find my friend and get out of here."

"You mean your boyfriend."

She did a double take as heat rose up in her cheeks.

Trevor smiled. "It's nice you have a boyfriend. It's about time you do something nice for yourself, Miss M."

She let out a laugh and shook her head. If only he knew. The levity in the moment of tension was most welcome. She was seeing before her the real Trevor, just a boy. A scared boy.

Sierra thought for a moment. She tugged on Trevor's shoulder. "Let's sneak out the back. The car is hidden down the road. Joseph is probably somewhere between the cabin and the car, looking for me." Or else something bad had happened to him.

She did a quick survey of the area around the back door. The trees came up nearly to the welcome mat. She raced toward the cover of the forest, with Trevor close behind her.

She ran deeper into the thick of the evergreens before turning and heading downhill. They darted out into a clearing just as she heard the zing of a rifle shot. She dropped to the ground and crawled toward the trees that were less than ten feet away. The sniper was still watching, ready to take a shot.

She reached the edge of the forest. Slipping behind the cover of a large tree trunk, she glanced sideways. Trevor had gone in a different direction to avoid the rifle shot. Probably deeper into the forest.

She heard footsteps from downhill. When she turned, Baseball Hat man lunged toward her.

"You keep getting away from me." He reached out for her.

She angled right, seeking to go deeper into the trees. If she went back out into the clearing, the sniper would line up another shot on her.

The man grabbed at her shirttail. She whirled around, swinging her arms wildly. She managed to slap him in the face, but it only stunned him. He reached for her neck. She twisted and kicked him hard in the shin.

He grimaced in pain, then clamped his hands around her neck. She struggled for breath even as she tried to break free of his viselike grip.

"Get off her." Trevor ran out of the trees and jumped on the man's back.

Any doubt she had about Trevor's loyalty was erased. Baseball Hat man turned his rage on Trevor. The two wrestled and rolled on the ground. The skinny kid was no match for the brawny man.

She glanced around, looking for a weapon.

She picked up a thick stick and smacked against Baseball Hat's back. The man yowled in pain.

He turned on her. She swung the stick again, but he dodged out of the way. Baseball Hat dove for the stick, yanking it out of her hand. He stomped toward her as she walked backward.

Swaying from side to side, Trevor pushed himself to his feet.

Baseball Hat lifted the stick to hit her.

"Run, Trevor," she said.

"I'm not leaving you, Miss M."

Though he was a foot shorter than Baseball Hat, Trevor lunged at the larger man, pushing on his back. The man whirled around and hit Trevor across the jaw with the stick. Trevor stumbled backward.

Rage surged through Sierra. What kind of a man would strike a kid like that?

She hit the man's back with her fists, knowing that it would provoke him. The man swung the stick at her.

"I'm getting tired of this." A voice came through the trees. Joseph came up behind the man and hit him on the head with a pistol. The man crumpled to the ground.

Joseph tilted his head toward Trevor. "What's his game?"

"He's all right." She gazed at Trevor, whose eyes watered from being hit so hard.

"Where is his sister?"

"She's in a safe place," said Trevor. "We need to go get her, though."

"Let's get out of here, then. This guy is going to come to in a matter of minutes." Joseph took off running. Sierra and Trevor fell in behind him. They pushed their way through the trees until they came to the car.

Joseph jumped behind the driver's seat. She got in the passenger side while Trevor climbed into the back.

Joseph backed the car out from the grove of trees that made the car less visible from the road. He turned the wheel so the car faced downhill.

The car had rolled only a short distance when a rifle shot shattered the side window. The sniper had taken aim.

Sierra slipped down in the seat, as did Joseph. He kept his head just above the dashboard so he could see to steer.

"Trevor, are you okay?"

The silence seemed to go on forever.

"Yes, I'm okay," came a faint voice from the back seat.

She let out a breath. The car started to fishtail.

"He hit the rear tires." Joseph spoke through gritted teeth. "Let's take this thing as far as we can."

The car rumbled and bumped to a stop. All of them crouched low in the seats. Joseph peered around. "He must be shooting from that ridge over there. Let's get out of the car on my side and head toward the trees."

Joseph pushed open the door and rolled out. Sierra scooted across the seat and crouched down beside him. A moment later, Trevor's door opened. His face was drained of color, and his eyes were wild.

She gave Trevor's shoulder a reassuring squeeze.

"I called the sheriff. They should be on their way up the mountain," said Sierra.

"Good. Let's see if you can get down this mountain alive and meet up with them," said Joseph.

Trevor still looked shell-shocked. "I never meant for this to happen. These guys are the big time. Way more dangerous than anybody I ever dealt with before."

"I know, Trevor." She locked him in her gaze. "What we've got to focus on now is getting out of here. Are you with me?"

The boy nodded.

"Let's head for those trees. They'll provide us with cover." The calm in Joseph's voice helped quell some of the terror Sierra battled.

Her feet pounded the hard ground as they

darted toward the thick of the forest. Joseph took the lead, and she fell in behind him. Trevor lagged, staring at the ground. She slowed so he could catch up.

Sierra glanced over her shoulder at the high spot where the sniper probably was.

They weren't out of danger yet, and she still had to find a way to get both Trevor and Daisy to a safe place.

As they approached an area where the trees didn't provide much cover, Joseph signaled to the others to drop to the ground. They crawled along at a snail's pace.

"Stay spread out," he commanded. The closer together they were, the more it would be like shooting fish in a barrel.

The rifle shot zinged in the air just in front of him. On the ridge off to his side, the metal of the rifle glinted in the noonday sun a couple hundred yards away.

There were other high spots where the sniper might move closer so they would still be in range. They wouldn't be totally safe until they met up with the sheriff.

He ran toward a cluster of trees. Sierra had wrapped an arm around Trevor to hurry him along. All three of them slumped to the ground to catch their breath.

"How much longer?" Trevor's voice was a monotone, and he had a dazed look in his eyes.

They hiked down the mountain, staying in the trees. A vehicle that sounded like a diesel truck went by on the road. Joseph caught a flash of color through the trees. The truck was rolling along slowly as if searching for something. The truck did not have the Sheriff's emblem on it. More men must have come to look for them.

Sierra shot him a fearful glance. Trevor's eyes were glazed as he stared straight ahead.

Joseph signaled for them to move deeper into the forest. On the road, the diesel engine stopped. A door slammed.

They quickened the pace until they were all sprinting downhill.

The trees thinned, and they emerged from the forest with the crossroads in sight. Down below, he spotted the sheriff's clearly marked SUV. They jogged toward the car.

Joseph gave a backward glance up the mountain. The deputy stopped at the crossroads and got out. They weren't likely to be followed now.

Joseph approached the deputy, who smiled at him. "You folks ran into some trouble?"

"Our car broke down is all."

The deputy tilted his head and looked at Sierra. "I thought the woman who phoned in said something about a potentially dangerous situation."

Though the sheriff's department was separate from the city police, Joseph was wary of involving them. Cops talked to each other.

"We just needed to get this kid. He's been in a little trouble. We weren't sure what we were facing," Sierra said.

She must understand the need to not give up too much information.

"Let me give you a ride back into town, then." The deputy pushed himself off the car and rubbed his chin. "All the same, we'll send somebody up there to have a look around."

The deputy wasn't totally buying their story. Joseph was concerned about his cover being blown on another level, as well. After so many encounters, the thugs must wonder where he got his self-defense skills. He hoped he just looked like a guy trying to protect his girlfriend.

Trevor got into the front seat, and Sierra and Joseph squeezed into the back with the bags of gear that rested on the seat. Their shoulders were touching. Both of them were still catching their breath from the run down the mountain.

The deputy glanced over at Trevor. "Are you okay? You look like you're about to throw up."

Joseph leaned forward and squeezed Trevor's shoulder. "He had a little scare is all."

Trevor lifted his head, seeming to shake himself free of the shock he'd experienced. "I'm fine. Okay?" His tone was defensive.

"Where can I take you folks?"

"My place?" Sierra recited her address. She gave Joseph a nervous glance. "The shop was supposed to drop off my car."

She must have some sort of plan she couldn't share with the deputy in the car. Though it was broad daylight, Joseph had reservations about even going to Sierra's house. Protection wouldn't be in place for her until tonight.

Joseph breathed a sigh of relief when the edge of Scenic View could be seen. Once they were among people, they weren't likely to be hunted down.

The deputy dropped them off in front of Sierra's house, which wasn't a house at all, but a grain silo on a plot of land. The nearest neighbor lived in a single-wide trailer down the road a bit.

Joseph stared at the round house with rose-bushes in front of it. "This is where you live?"

"Yes, what did you think?"

Joseph shrugged. "That you would live in a smaller version of your father's house."

"My father and I live very different lives," she said. Her expression grew serious as she drew her eyebrows together. "I've taken care of myself since I got sober. I love my father, but I don't have anything to do with him or his money."

His own insecurity about his upbringing below the poverty line had caused him to make assumptions about her. He stared at her house. "It certainly is different."

"I think her house is the bomb. She did a lot of the work herself." Trevor seemed to be coming back to life.

"Trevor, we have to go get Daisy." She turned to face Joseph. "Is there any way we can get these kids into some kind of protective custody?"

"I can make some calls. We can get something temporary set up fairly quickly."

"That's fine, but they will need something permanent. New names and foster parents."

"Can I ask why?" Joseph put his hands on his hips.

"The dealers threatened Daisy's life if Trevor didn't do what they said," said Sierra.

Trevor stepped closer to them. "You mean I won't get to say goodbye to Margaret? She's been a good foster mom to me and Daisy."

"Trevor, we can't take that chance." Her voice softened when the boy's shoulders slumped. "Maybe you can give her a call when we get you to a safe place."

"We'll do the best we can," Joseph said.

Trevor pressed his lips together and then stared at the ground. He shrugged. "I guess that's how it has to be." He cut a glance toward Sierra. "What's up with your boyfriend, anyway? I thought he ran the skateboard shop."

She glanced nervously at Joseph. "Are you ready to take us to Daisy now?" Sierra's words were filled with compassion. "That's what we need to focus on."

Though Joseph appreciated Sierra's diversionary tactic, Trevor was clearly figuring out something was up. That was fine, as long as he got Trevor out of town before he had the chance to tell anyone else.

Trevor shoved his hands in his pockets and kicked the dirt. "Yeah, I can do that."

Sierra walked toward the car. Remembering the bomb that had destroyed his storefront, Joseph grabbed her arm. "Give me a second to check the car out."

He crawled underneath the car, opened the trunk and checked the wheel wells. Sierra wrapped an arm around Trevor. "He's just being cautious."

"I heard about the explosion at the store," said Trevor.

"Okay, it checks out. You drive so I can start making some calls."

Once Joseph was in the passenger seat, Sierra buckled up and turned toward Trevor in the back seat. "Where is she?"

"She's in the park with the homeless people."

"That's a heck of a hiding place, Trevor."

"They move around. Some of them go to the library during the day or down to the soup kitchen."

"We'll check the park first," said Sierra.

Joseph got on his phone, making calls to set up some sort of temporary safe housing for Trevor and his sister until they could get them into witness protection. After several calls, he turned to Sierra. "We can get them on a plane tonight. A DEA agent will meet them in Seattle. They'll text me a photo of him so Trevor and his sister will know who to look for."

Sierra glanced over at him. "Thank you. I couldn't have done this without you." She lifted her head. "Does that sound good, Trevor?"

"Wait a second. I heard the conversation he had on the phone. This guy is a cop," said Trevor. "Is he even your boyfriend?"

Sierra gave Joseph a wry smile. A charge of electricity passed between them. "You'll never know, Trevor."

Joseph liked the way light came into her blue eyes just then.

Sierra drove through downtown Scenic View, taking several turns on her way to the park.

Twice he glanced in the rearview mirror to see a white truck behind them.

Sierra's gaze bounced from the mirror to him to the street in front of her. She must have noticed the truck, too.

Sierra turned on the street that led to the park. Joseph prayed it was just a coincidence that the white truck had taken the exit, as well.

TEN

Sierra circled around the edge of the park. "Do you see her anywhere, Trevor?"

Trevor shook his head. "No, but Old Bart is there on his spot on the bench. He sees everything that goes on."

Sierra wasn't crazy about getting out of the car and walking through the park. She'd hoped this would be an easy pickup so they could get out of here as fast as possible.

Joseph leaned across the seat and patted her hand. "It'll be all right."

She pushed open the door. "Let's make this quick."

Old Bart was probably no more than fifty years of age. He'd been a fixture in Scenic View for at least ten years. He wore ragged shorts and his trademark Dallas Cowboys shirt. He had a paper bag filled with seeds that he threw out for the birds.

Sierra watched the white truck she'd noticed

earlier pull in along the street by the park. The driver remained behind the wheel. Her heart beat a little faster.

Trevor ran ahead to question Old Bart. Sierra watched as Old Bart shook his head and threw out a handful of seeds to the gathering pigeons. Trevor trotted toward another group of people who sat in a circle while one of them played guitar.

When she looked back at the white truck, the driver was no longer behind the wheel. She glanced around at the people in the park, paying attention to the younger, muscular men. Any one of them could have gotten out of that white truck.

Maybe it was just a coincidence that the truck had followed them to the park. Still, she felt vulnerable out here in the open. Joseph stood close to her, his gaze darting everywhere.

Trevor trotted back toward them. "They said they saw her about twenty minutes ago. She was headed toward Boulder Beach."

"Where is that?" Joseph continued to survey the park for threats.

Sierra turned and pointed. "It's across the street bordering the lake."

Joseph squeezed her arm. "I'll get the car turned around and pulled up to the street so we can get out of here as fast as possible."

She handed him the keys, then she and Trevor crossed the street. They stood at the edge of the road, staring down at an expanse of rocks decreasing in size as they got closer to the shore. There were several clusters of people close to the water's edge. Some floated or swam out in the water.

She searched for Daisy's blond head.

"There." Trevor pointed at a small figure sitting on a flat boulder with a book in her hand. She was some distance from the other people at the far end of the beach.

A man wearing a jacket walked along the beach. He looked at each person there as though searching. It was too warm to be wearing a coat. Was he hiding a gun?

Calling Daisy's name would only draw attention to her.

"Let's get down there." A sense of urgency fueled Sierra's movements. Trevor had found a very clever way to hide his sister in plain sight, but Sierra did not want to take any chances.

They crawled over some of the rocks and around others.

"Daisy!" Trevor shouted.

Sierra tugged on Trevor's sleeve. "The less we say her name the better, Trevor."

Daisy turned, her face brightening when she saw her brother. She was a petite waif of a child with bright round eyes and hair the color of straw.

The man in the jacket was now moving toward her, increasing his pace. She could see clearly now that he was the man who had threatened her at the skateboard shop. He wouldn't shoot with witnesses around, but he could use the gun to abduct Daisy if he got close enough to press it against her.

Sierra signaled frantically for Daisy to come toward them. She slipped off the rock, a look of confusion clouding her face.

Sierra hurried to get to the child before the man did. Navigating around the rocks slowed her progress. Daisy turned and saw the man coming toward her. She whirled around and hurried up the rocky hillside. Panic etched her features as she glanced at Trevor and then Sierra.

"That man is going after her." Trevor was out of breath.

Sierra rushed ahead of Trevor. She reached her hand out toward Daisy. The girl's delicate hand slipped into Sierra's.

Sierra looked over her shoulder up at the street as she pulled Daisy toward safety. Joseph had parked the car at the curb.

"Trevor, get up to the car as fast as you can."

The man glanced over at the crowds with his

hands on his hips. He wouldn't be able to shoot and escape quickly. The man pulled a phone out of his pocket.

Daisy squeezed Sierra's hand a little tighter. "What's happening, Miss M?"

"We're going to get you and your brother to a safe place."

Joseph got out of the car and opened the doors. Trevor slid into the back seat. Sierra let go of Daisy's hand only once she was safely in the car.

Sierra sat in the front passenger seat while Joseph got behind the wheel.

Joseph glanced over at her. "You look a little shook up. Any trouble?"

"We managed." She clicked her seat belt into place. "But I think he called in reinforcements." She pressed her head back against the seat, trying to catch her breath.

Joseph put his hand on hers. "You made it."

His touched warmed her to the bone and calmed her down.

Joseph pulled out onto the street.

"I saw that guy," said Trevor. "How could they have found out about Daisy?"

"One of the homeless people must have ratted me out," said Daisy. "I tried to stay away from the junkies, but that's not easy. Where are we going?"

"To the airport," said Trevor.

"You mean we have to leave Scenic View and Margaret?" Daisy's voice filled with anguish.

Sierra turned to face the two kids in the back seat.

Trevor patted his sister's shoulder. "It's the only way, Daisy. I'm sorry I got us into so much trouble."

Tears formed in Daisy's eyes.

"We'll have quite a wait at the airport. There will be time to call your foster mom and say goodbye," Joseph said.

"Why can't we go by her house and say goodbye? I want to see her and hug her one last time." Daisy crossed her arms over her chest and stuck out her lower lip.

"It's too dangerous for both of you," Joseph said.

Sierra's heart broke for both Trevor and Daisy. They'd been shuffled around their whole life, with only each other to depend on, and now they were being uprooted again. "Where you're going, you'll be safe. Those men won't be able to hurt you or make Trevor do bad things."

"You didn't see a man with a large-faced watch in the forest that night Sierra came to get you, did you?" Joseph asked.

Trevor shook his head. "No, I never saw anyone like that."

Joseph said, "Which way to the airport?"

"Scenic View only has a private airport. We need to drive to Grotto Falls."

Joseph took the next exit and headed out first on a two-lane road and then on the highway. Fields of wheat, cows, sheep and farmhouses passed by in a blur.

The sound of Daisy crying softly and Trevor comforting her made Sierra's own heart ache. Each kid was such an important part of her life. "I'm going to miss you guys."

Joseph reached over and squeezed her hand. The show of support, the tenderness of his touch renewed her sense of purpose. They were in this together, getting these kids to safety and a better life.

The signs indicated the exit for the airport on the outskirts of Grotto Falls.

Joseph followed the signs to short-term parking and stopped the car. "Got more than a few hours before your flight."

"Where are we going?"

"Seattle. A man will meet you there and help you get settled. Trevor, he might have some questions for you."

"Who is he?" Daisy leaned forward.

"He's a DEA agent like me," said Joseph. "He's tall and has hair like Albert Einstein. I'll show you a picture."

"Wait a second," said Daisy. "You mean you are not Miss M's boyfriend?"

"I'll explain later." Trevor tugged on his sister's sleeve, and they both got out of the car.

Trevor and Daisy walked ahead of Joseph and Sierra.

"Stay close, guys." Sierra's nerves were on edge. The muscular man with the big teeth had been talking to someone on the phone when they left Scenic View. "Did you notice anyone following us?"

"No, but that doesn't mean anything. As long as we keep the kids in the public areas of the airport, we should be okay."

She rolled her eyes. "Getting teenagers to do what you say is kind of like herding cats."

Joseph laughed. "I'm sure we'll do just fine." His eyes shone with admiration as he winked at her.

She liked that he used the word "we."

Once inside the airport they stayed together, visiting the shops, eating a burger and sitting. The kids made a tearful phone call to Margaret. Sierra could not shake the feeling that they were being watched. She caught Joseph surveying the shops and seating areas.

Joseph patted her shoulder. "It's getting close. I'll go get the boarding passes."

She watched him stride over to a kiosk. He had a confident, easy gait.

Daisy sat next to her while Trevor lay on the carpet on his stomach, reading a book she had bought for him. Sierra flipped through a magazine.

Daisy rested her chin on Sierra's shoulder. "I'm bored out of my mind. Can I just go over to that shop over there?"

Daisy pointed at a shop across the carpet that looked like it sold sweaters and handbags.

"I suppose that would be okay. Stay where I can see you."

Daisy leaped up and trotted over to the shop. Sierra watched as she held up a sweater that was way too big for her and made a face. She laughed and then glanced down at her magazine.

"Your sister's being funny, Trevor."

A moment later he looked up from his book. "Where? I don't see her."

Fear zinged through her like a bullet. She'd looked away for only a second. But she couldn't see Daisy's blond head anywhere in the shop.

Heart pounding, Sierra shot to her feet and raced toward the display of sweaters. Tension invaded every muscle in her body as she paced through the shop, peering behind a tall display of handbags. Her gaze bounced all around the airport shops, to the exits and the seating areas. No Daisy.

She came to the threshold of the shop and peered out to where Trevor and now Joseph were standing.

She took in a shallow breath and shook her head.

They both pointed at the same time. A tall man stepped out of the way, revealing Daisy standing in line at the frozen yogurt store. Trevor and Joseph had been able to see her from where they stood.

Sierra rushed over to her. "You scared me half to death."

"Sorry, I was hungry. I thought you would see me going over here."

She waited while Daisy got her yogurt.

Joseph and Sierra walked Daisy and Trevor to the security line. Sierra hugged both of them as her throat went tight.

"I can show my ID and make sure they are safe on the plane. I'll check out the rest of the passengers, just as a precaution," Joseph said.

As they moved through the line, Joseph's phone rang.

Daisy broke away and ran back to give Sierra one more hug.

"You take care of each other." Tears formed in Sierra's eyes.

"Miss M, I know Joseph is just your pretend boyfriend. Trevor explained it to me, but the way he looks at you—" Daisy stood on tiptoe so she could whisper in Sierra's ear. "I think he likes you. Everyone in youth group thinks it's high time you got a boyfriend." Daisy ran back to join her brother, who had cut out of line to wait for her with Joseph beside him. She whirled around and waved at Sierra. The two kids disappeared as the line progressed.

Daisy's comment had left Sierra reeling. Did the youth group kids, her kids, talk about her love life, or lack of one?

Joseph came back through security and stood beside her. "You look upset. Is everything okay?"

She turned to face him. His dark brown eyes seemed to twinkle. "Just something Daisy said." Did a thirteen-year-old kid see something she wasn't willing to acknowledge?

He shook his head and leaned closer to her. She could smell the soapy cleanness of his skin. "What do you mean?"

After she'd pulled herself from addiction with God's help, she had decided to dedicate her time to helping other kids not fall into the same abyss. She feared that she just wasn't good at picking men. Her life had felt full, but now, as she stared into Joseph's eyes, as the softness of his smile warmed her to the bone, she began to wonder if maybe there was something missing in her life.

"Just an issue I need to work through."

Maybe there was a part of her that thought she didn't deserve a man as good as Joseph.

"I'm sure you'll figure it out." His voice touched her in a way that made her heart beat faster.

Realization snapped her free of the sensation that she was melting in her shoes. She took a step back, pulling away from the force field that attraction created. She liked and respected Joseph, but he would be leaving Scenic View as soon as the man she'd seen in the woods was caught. Why set herself up for heartbreak?

He held up his phone. "That was the agent in Seattle just confirming things. The kids will be okay."

"We should get back to town." She managed a very businesslike tone, though his comment made her feel the loss of Trevor and Daisy all over again.

Joseph lifted his head and glanced around at the clusters of people. "Yes, let's get moving."

As they walked toward the exit, Joseph placed a protective hand on the middle of her back. His touch sent an electric charge through her at the same time she felt pain over what could never be. They were two different people from two very different worlds.

They stepped outside into the darkness. The plane that probably held Daisy and Trevor took off, cutting through the sky at an extreme angle.

Joseph got behind the wheel and she buckled herself into the passenger seat. Once they were away from the airport and out on the highway, Sierra stared up at the starry sky. Didn't Joseph say her extra protection would be here tonight? She was looking forward to a long soak in her tub and sleeping in her own bed.

They left the highway and turned onto the two-lane road that led to Scenic View.

Joseph sat up a little straighter. "We've got company." His voice remained calm, though she detected the undercurrent of fear.

She craned her neck to see headlights nearly blinding her. The other car loomed dangerously close on the empty road.

ELEVEN

Joseph gripped the wheel a little tighter as he pressed the gas pedal to the floor. He felt a surge of energy in the face of such danger. His focus heightened, and his brain cleared. This is what he was born to do.

He glanced over at Sierra, who gripped the armrest. This was not what she was born to do.

"Hang in there. I got this," he said, keeping his voice calm.

The car stayed on their bumper. Maybe the driver was just someone who got a thrill out of following too close, but he doubted it. They'd probably been followed from Scenic View. Traffic had been heavy and the tail hadn't had an opportunity to get to them on the way to the airport. But now, in the darkness of the night, they were the only two cars on the road.

Sierra gazed at him for a long moment before glancing over her shoulder.

He'd felt a spark pass between them earlier

at the airport. The heat had ruled his emotions for only a moment. He was in Scenic View to do a job. He reminded himself that the number one rule of undercover work was not to form attachments.

"What should we do?" Terror permeated her voice.

Their car topped out at about eighty. He couldn't make it go any faster. "Let's just stay the course."

They entered a canyon. The road became curvier and the drop-off rocky and extreme. He hugged the inside of the curve as he turned the wheel. The other car, some sort of sports model, handled the curves with more agility.

It tapped their bumper just as they hit a straight patch of road. Their car shook from the impact but remained on the road.

The other car pulled up beside them on the two-lane. It was too dark to see the other driver. The car eased sideways toward them. The mountain that the road had been cut through filled Sierra's window. Up ahead, a set of headlights loomed toward them as a car appeared around a curve. The sports car dropped back behind them.

The car coming in the opposite direction whizzed past them.

The sports car hit their bumper twice. Joseph

veered into the other lane, coming close to the edge of the steep drop-off. Adrenaline surged through his body as he turned the wheel to get back into his own lane.

Sierra gripped the armrest and pressed her head against the seat.

A sign flashed a warning that the road up ahead was curvy and that they needed to slow down. The other car remained glued to their back end.

Sierra checked her seat belt.

He couldn't slow down. The yellow lines on the highway zoomed by. He maneuvered into the curve and out of it as another serpentine curve loomed in front of him.

His pulse drummed in his ears. He felt like he was enveloped in a bubble as he focused on keeping his speed up and hugging the winding road. The car bumped them again, this time with more force.

His car was propelled into the opposite lane. He careened back toward the rocky cliff. Their car swerved, crossing the yellow dividing line and then back over. The crunch of metal on metal surrounded him. The steep drop-off drew nearer. The front tires slipped over the edge. Their car flipped at an angle and rolled twice landing parallel to the road.

Sierra screamed.

The car groaned and screeched and then landed upright. The windshield looked like tiny irregular diamonds. The roof was bent.

His body felt like he'd gone ten rounds with a prize fighter. He glanced over at Sierra, who rested her palm on her chest as if she were trying to slow her own heartbeat.

The headlights of the other car shone just above the rim of the drop-off.

Her side of the car was the closest to the road. She shielded her eyes from the glare of the headlights. "I'm all right," she said.

Joseph took in a deep breath, hoping to slow down his own pounding heart. He peered through Sierra's window at the menacing headlights. "He's probably not going to leave until he's sure he's finished us off."

Time seem to stand still in the bubble of false safety. The driver hadn't gotten out of the car, and yet he hadn't left.

"We can't stay here forever," Sierra groaned. "I'm pretty beat up from the crash, but nothing is screaming in pain. I don't think anything is broken."

"We're going to have to make a run for it." He stared down at the dark landscape below them—a cluster of trees and an open field.

"Why doesn't he get out of the car? Or take

a shot at us, something?" Her voice filled with fear. "Why is he tormenting us like this?"

Their headlights were off, and there was no light inside their car. At best, they would be shadows to the assassin. He was probably waiting for them to exit the car so his headlights would reveal their position.

Joseph pushed on the door. It creaked. The metal screeched but it didn't open. "The roof is too bent on my side. I can't get my door open."

"He'll shoot if we go out on my side." She unclicked her seat belt before glancing up the incline. "Can we crawl out through the back on your side?"

Joseph had the sensation that a clock was ticking. The man who had run them off the road was taking delight in knowing that they were trapped. Once they left the car, they would be easy targets.

Sierra angled her body and tried to slip over the front seat.

He freed himself from his seat belt. The roof of the car was bent in such a way that he could turn around only partly. "I can't get turned around in here. I'm a lot bigger than you," he said.

Sierra spoke to him from the back seat, taking nervous glances up the hill. "I can crawl out this way. Maybe I can get your door open from the outside."

The car would provide her with cover. If the man intended to shoot them, he would have to come down the hill to get a shot at her. Still, she would be exposed and Joseph would be trapped inside. He touched his gun in the shoulder holster. Could he hold off the assassin from inside the car while she tried to pry the door open?

"I don't know, Sierra. It's risky. The roof is really crushed." He couldn't put her in that kind of danger.

"Can you slip over to my side of the car and crawl back that way?"

Sierra was a petite, thin woman and she had the agility of a gymnast. "I'll give it a shot." He pulled his phone out of his pocket and texted his handler his position and situation.

"Is this the best time to be texting?"

"Just something I need to take care of." Though he didn't want to scare Sierra, sending such a message was his way of letting his handler know he was pretty sure he was in a situation he wouldn't get out of alive. The DEA would at least know where to search for his body.

"Give it a shot, Joseph. Climb over." He could barely make out her features in the dim light. The note of hope in her voice broke his heart.

Even if he had to die here, was there some way he could get her to safety?

"Can you make a run for it?" He pulled his gun from its holster and eased over to the passenger seat.

"No, Joseph. He'll shoot you for sure."

He stretched across the seat to where she'd been sitting and rolled down the window slowly. "I'm giving you an order, Sierra."

"You can't do that. This isn't the army." She reached forward and tugged on his sleeve. "Please, Joseph. I don't want you to die."

He gripped her hand. "When I start shooting, you run. There is no reason why both of us need to die." He spoke through gritted teeth.

She shook her head. "I won't leave you."

He rolled the window down far enough to brace his handgun on the rim. "Stay in line with the car so it provides you with cover until you can get to those trees. Run, I said."

His first shot took out a headlight.

Sierra pushed open the door on the downhill side of the car. Her voice filled with frustration. "I don't want to do this."

At least now she saw the situation for what it was.

He lined up his sight to take out the other headlight just as a door of the sports car squeaked open and slammed shut. He said a quick prayer and pulled the trigger.

Sierra hit the ground when she heard the second shot. A third shot reverberated through the night…a different sound, from the assassin's gun.

She lay on her stomach, tearing at the grass. The shelter of the trees was some ten yards away. She couldn't do this. She couldn't leave Joseph to die.

She burst to her feet and ran parallel to the road. Maybe she could flank the assassin and jump on him from behind while his attention was on Joseph.

More shots were fired. Glass shattered. Judging from where the shot had come from, the assassin had worked his way a few yards down the rocky incline, using a large boulder for cover.

Silence enveloped her like a shroud. The seconds ticked by. She couldn't see any movement within the car. No silhouette of Joseph. He might be crouching low in the passenger seat… and he might be dead. Her breath caught.

The assassin lifted his head above the rim of the rock and then ducked back down. His head was more moving shadows than distinct features. There was no response from Joseph in the car, no movement. Her heart squeezed tight. Was he dead?

Crouching low, she took a few steps toward the road, choosing her path carefully so as not to make any noise. The silence of the night was oppressive. Her pulse drummed in her ears. She had the sensation of being underwater...of time slowing down. She focused in on the wrecked car, looking for anything that might indicate Joseph was okay.

The passenger side door of the car clicked open. It was too dark to see the door opening, but she'd heard it.

She let out the breath she'd been holding. Joseph was alive. An emotion that went deeper than relief permeated her awareness. No matter how hard she tried to keep it from happening, the affection she felt for Joseph had gone so much deeper than friendship.

As far as she knew, the assassin was still behind the rock toward the front end of her car. Joseph was between her and the shooter.

She saw Joseph's lighter colored sneakers as he slipped to the ground. His back was to her. He must be intending to use the door as a shield. He had no way of knowing she had come back to help him. And she couldn't let him know without the assassin hearing her, too.

Her own breathing seemed to surround her

as she stood frozen. She peered up the incline. What if she made a run for the other car? The assassin was still closer to the car than either she or Joseph was. Would Joseph be able to hold the assassin off and make it to the road?

Joseph raised his gun so it rested on the window. He took a shot and ducked behind the door. The assassin raised his head and took a shot. Joseph fired back.

Now was her chance to try to get to the car, while they were distracted, fighting each other. She raced up the incline. Rocks cascaded down the hill, crashing into each other and alerting both men of her position. She dropped to the ground and crawled toward the shelter of a larger rock.

Joseph turned and looked in her direction. In the dark, he probably couldn't pinpoint her exact location. At least he knew she hadn't left him to die.

She rose. Still crouching, she took a few more careful steps up the hill. Now she was in a straight line with the rock where the assassin had taken cover. The car with its headlights shot out appeared as a silhouette above her.

A shot reverberated around her, so close it felt like her eardrum had been hit with a hammer. She squeezed her eyes shut. She said a quick prayer, then crouched low but kept moving uphill, knowing that the darkness would shield her as long as she was quiet.

Another shot was fired. This one from Joseph's gun. She glanced across the expanse of rock to see a shadow headed up toward the road. Then Joseph darted out from behind the car door, moving only a few feet to take cover behind the same rock the assassin had been behind. Or so she thought. She couldn't see much, but heard footsteps and rocks hitting each other as they rolled downhill.

She hurried up toward the rim of the road.

The assassin got to the car first. He fired a shot at her. She retreated back down the hill and fell to the rocky ground.

Silence descended. Still lying on her stomach, she swallowed and pressed her lips together, listening…waiting.

Up above her, she heard the noise of the assassin circling the car on the asphalt.

She heard footsteps off to the side. Joseph was coming toward her. He touched her arm.

"I don't have any bullets left. Let's get up there before he reloads. It's two against one."

That might be true, but the one had a gun.

In the silence and the dark, they scrambled up the rocky incline.

The assassin came around the side of the car

and fired off two shots. Both of them hit the ground. Joseph covered her body with his.

The seconds ticked by. They heard footsteps on the road. The assassin paced, trying to figure out where they were in the dark.

Sierra's heart pounded.

Then the car engine started up. The assassin backed the car away from the road and sped away. The sound of his car engine grew fainter.

Joseph rolled away from her. He shook his head. "What just happened?"

Another set of headlights appeared at the rim of the road. The motor of the truck above them made a noise like an old-fashioned washing machine.

A woman's voice sounded above them. "You folks look like you've been in an accident. Can I give you a hand?"

So the assassin had been scared off by an approaching Good Samaritan. Sierra took in a deep breath as a sense of peace surrounded her.

Joseph got to his feet and reached out a hand to help Sierra up, as well. "Boy, are we glad to see you." He held on to her hand as they made their way back up to the road. When they got to the top of it, he still held her hand. Her small hand fit snugly into his. She could feel the calluses and the strength in his fingers. She squeezed his hand.

Holding it felt like the most natural thing in the world. As the woman stepped toward them, Sierra shot Joseph a quick glance. He squeezed her fingers.

He had shown he was willing to give up his life for her and she for him.

The woman walked with a little bit of a limp. Her wild white hair stuck out from beneath a cowboy hat. Her truck looked like it was from the 1950s.

She held out a hand to Joseph. "Name's Della, but everyone just calls me Dell. I own an organic farm and honey operation just up the road a piece." She glanced down at their wrecked car. "I'd say that's toast." She leaned a little closer to them as if to see their faces. "What happened? Did a deer surprise you?"

"Something like that," said Joseph.

"You got to watch out for those critters at nighttime."

"Yes, those critters. They'll get you every time."

She gave Joseph a knowing glance. He still held her hand.

"Well, come on and get into my rig. I'll take you wherever you need to go." She pointed toward a bloodhound in the bed of the truck. "Don't mind Jasper. He won't hurt you. He's as sweet as the day is long." Her voice had a slow drawl to it.

They climbed into the cab of the truck, with Sierra in the middle and Joseph by the passenger door.

The truck rumbled down the road into the night, its headlights showing the yellow lines ticking by and cutting a swath of illumination that revealed only a hint of the fields and barbed wire fences they drove past.

Sierra gave one backward glance through the window.

They were safe for now.

But the car without the headlights—and the assassin who had run them off the road—were still out there.

TWELVE

As they drew near to the outskirts of Scenic View, Joseph's phone vibrated. The text was from Sierra's female protection. The first one had been sent hours ago. DEA agent Cindy Sloan had been waiting for him at the shop for several hours.

"Can you drop us off on Bowman Street outside the skateboard shop?"

"Sure thing, partner," said Dell.

Dell drove through town and braked in front of the shop. Though the storefront was dark, the display window had been replaced. He was going to have to get back to the job that provided him with his cover.

"Thanks for the ride, Dell," said Sierra. "Nice talking to you."

The door of the old pickup creaked and screeched as Joseph pushed it open.

Dell pulled away from the curb on the quiet street. Stars twinkled in the night sky.

"Why are we stopping here?" Sierra glanced up at the abandoned street.

There were several vehicles parked within a four-block radius of the skateboard shop. She was probably thinking the same thing he was. Chances were, the shop was being watched.

"Your extra protection is waiting for you. I left a key hidden for her. She's waiting in the office," he said.

They circled around to the alley, and he opened the door. A forty-something woman sat with a suitcase beside her. She had a laptop open on the desk.

He had met Cindy Sloan on a previous operation. She was a no-nonsense single mom with two teenage kids, a boy and girl. Though he hadn't worked closely with her, she had a reputation for being a good agent.

Cindy lifted her fingers from the keyboard and offered them a faint smile.

"Sorry about the delay. We got held up, so to speak," Joseph said.

"No problem." Cindy glanced back at her keyboard. "It allowed me to get caught up on some paperwork on another case."

"Cindy, this is Sierra Monforton."

Sierra stepped toward Cindy and held out her hand. Cindy stood up and shook it.

"I assume you came by car," Joseph said.

"Yes, it's parked in the alley."

He felt a sense of relief in seeing Cindy. It would be nice to have another agent to strategize with, and also good to know Sierra would be safe when he couldn't be around.

"Sierra will give you directions to her house. Both of us are beyond exhausted."

Cindy picked up the shoulder holster that held her gun.

"You won't be able to wear that once you make your appearance as Sierra's long-lost cousin."

"I know. But I will keep it close while I'm on guard duty at her house." Cindy patted the gun.

After slipping into her shoulder holster, Cindy grabbed her laptop and suitcase and stepped toward the door. "Let's get you home, Sierra." Her tone held a motherly quality.

Sierra looked at Cindy and then gazed at Joseph. "Well, I guess this is good-night." She seemed to want to say something more.

The moment felt awkward, too formal and cold for what they had been through in the previous hours.

"I'll be waiting by the car," said Cindy. She must have sensed their need for privacy. She stepped outside.

Sierra rushed across the room and wrapped

her arms around Joseph. "It feels strange leaving you."

He loved the way it felt to hold her in his arms. To be surrounded by the faint rose scent of her perfume. But it was wrong.

"You're in good hands with Cindy." Even as he felt a surge of attraction to her, his voice took on a businesslike tone. Whatever feelings had blossomed for her, he had to push them aside. It would be cruel to lead her on and let her think there could be something between them.

He wasn't the manager of a skateboard shop, and they weren't really a couple. He was a DEA agent on a case. She was a woman whose life was under threat. That was their reality.

She stepped back from the hug. Her blue eyes studied him. "Well, good night." A chill had entered her voice, as well.

Unable to absorb the pain he saw in her expression, he turned away and picked up some papers on his desk that didn't need to be straightened. "I'll catch up with you soon enough. We can work on putting together a composite of the guy you saw."

"Yeah, sure."

He still needed her help.

Sierra stepped through the door, closing it behind her.

It felt as though all the air had left the room.

Yes, he had feelings for her, but it was wrong to tease her or lead her on.

Fatigue settled into his muscles and bones like a heavy lead blanket. He clicked off the office light and headed toward the stairs that led to his apartment.

He was halfway up when he heard the screech of tires. He raced back down the stairs and out into the dark alley. Cindy lay on the ground on her side. She moved and groaned. Sierra was nowhere in sight.

He sprinted over to Cindy.

"Cindy?"

She touched the back of her head. "They hit me from behind."

He reached down to help get Cindy in a sitting position. "Sierra—where is she?"

Cindy was slow to respond. She moaned from the pain. "I'm not sure..."

He glanced up and down the alley. "They must have pushed her in a car and taken off."

Cindy pulled a set of keys out of her pocket. "Take my car. I'll be all right. I can get to the ER on my own to be checked out. But I'm in no condition to go with you." She pulled her gun from the holster. "Take this. You'll need it."

Joseph gave Cindy a reassuring pat on the back and then ran toward her car. He jumped in it and barreled down the alley and up the street.

He saw the taillights of the other car, already five blocks away and moving at a high speed.

Joseph pressed the gas pedal to the floor. He hung back. There was very little traffic out at this hour. He didn't want the person driving the car that held Sierra to know he was being tailed. He was grateful when another car emerged from a side street to serve as a buffer between himself and the car he was tailing.

The other car slowed down to the speed limit, probably not wanting to draw attention to itself. The car that held Sierra took the road that led to the marina, and parked in the lot that bordered it. Though there were lights on in some of the boats, there was no activity outside.

Joseph parked his car a block away so as not to draw attention to himself. He pushed the door open and got out, watching the parked car as he made his way through the parking lot, crouching and using the other cars for cover.

The car that contained Sierra remained parked. No lights came on. No doors opened. He drew in a shaky breath. Had they already killed her and were looking for an opportunity to drop her body?

Joseph hurried from car to car until he was three cars behind the one that held Sierra. Still no movement.

A light shone across the water in the distance,

a boat coming in to dock. He watched as the lights drew closer. The boat eased into a docking space.

The doors of the car opened and two men got out, one of them holding Sierra. Joseph waited until the men were on deck before moving in closer. Whoever had piloted the boat stayed below deck, not making an appearance.

One of the men took Sierra below deck while the other remained on deck watching.

The boat's motor started up.

He had only minutes to get on the boat, or Sierra would fall victim to whatever plan these men had. He waited for a moment's distraction from the guard on deck. The man held on to the railing and stared out at the parking lot, and then turned toward the water as the boat eased out of the dock.

Joseph leaped toward the side of the boat, catching hold of some hanging rope. He held on. Once they were away from the lights of the marina and the engine was running at full power, he would be harder to see and hear.

As the boat gained speed, he swung toward a window, catching a glimpse of Sierra sitting in a chair, her hands tied in front of her. Her head was turned. She didn't see him. He swung back. Joseph reached up and gripped the edge of the boat.

The lights of the marina faded in the distance.

He pulled himself up so the deck was at eye level. The guard had his back to Joseph. Joseph hoisted himself on deck, scrambling for the cover of a storage box. The boat was large enough to have a dinghy attached to it. That might provide a means of escape once he got Sierra free.

He suspected the plan was to find a secluded spot and dump Sierra in the water where her body might not be found, ever. He had no way of knowing if they would kill her first or just throw her overboard, weighting her body to guarantee she wouldn't escape. The possibility of that happening renewed his courage.

He had not had time to reload his gun since they'd been run off the road coming home from the airport. He was grateful for Cindy's gun. There were at least three men on board: the two who had kidnapped Sierra and whoever had brought the boat in. The odds were not good. He'd have to overpower the guard on deck, since gunfire would draw attention to his presence.

He watched and waited for his opportunity, knowing that time was not on his side for saving Sierra's life.

Sierra took in a deep breath. One of the men who had grabbed her was her old friend Baseball

Hat. The other man who had taken her outside Joseph's shop and now was assigned to guard her was probably no more than twenty years old. He was thin to the point of looking malnourished. Though he seemed coherent enough, his appearance and demeanor suggested he was a drug user. He paced back and forth in front of Sierra, ran his fingers through his greasy hair and rubbed his bare arms.

The way he held the gun in his hand, as though it were covered with a toxic substance, suggested he wasn't in the habit of using a firearm. Not like the assassins who had come after them.

This man pacing the room wasn't much older than the kids she worked with. Her heart swelled with compassion for him.

"Did they talk you into doing this?"

He turned to face her as though seeing her for the first time. "I owe a debt."

"And if you guard me, that takes care of the debt?"

"What do you care?" The man sat opposite her but bounced up from his chair almost as fast as he'd sat down.

She had a view of the watery landscape through her round window. She couldn't see any shoreline. They must be taking her to some place remote in the middle of the lake. She shuddered. Was this it? The last hour of her life was going to end out here in the depths of the lake? If they weighted her body, she would never be found.

She could think of no other reason they hadn't just killed her in the alley. They'd knocked Cindy out. And Joseph had still been in the office. Her heart ached for him. She hadn't thought she would ever care for a man like she cared for Joseph. Though he did not seem to return the affection. Now she felt foolish for hugging him in the office and gushing. Despite her best efforts, her heart had opened up to him.

She was alone and she was going to die. But she wasn't afraid of death.

She looked at the young man, who shifted his weight from foot to foot. "I do care. What is your name?"

If this was going to be her last hour on earth, she might as well make good use of it and extend some kindness to this young man.

The man sat down on the chair, but this time remained seated. "My name is Clive." Still holding the gun, he scratched his bare arms and looked off to the side.

"You know that they're probably going to kill me, right?"

Clive put up his hands. "I was just told to

watch you." A bit of guilt tinged his voice. "That's all I got to do."

"It doesn't have to be like this, Clive. You don't have to be tangled up with these kinds of people. I know people like you, just kids. I used to be like you. You make a couple of bad choices and then your life ends up in a place you never thought possible."

His expression hardened. "Quit it with the sob stories."

But she wasn't going to stop. She saw no way out of her inevitable death. Even if she could overpower Clive and jump overboard, they would come back and fish her out of the water. "I bet you had dreams once."

Above them, footsteps pounded louder and more intense than before. Both of them lifted their heads. There must be a guard posted on deck. It sounded like he was wrestling with something, moving it around.

Clive looked at her and shook his head. "Lady, you got to stop it." His voice lacked conviction. He shook his head and patted his forehead with his palm. "What am I doing here?"

"Look, I don't see a way out of this. I just wanted my last conversation on earth to be important. I'm glad it could be with you, Clive."

The granite-like hardness of his features seemed to soften for just a moment before the light left his eyes and he raised the gun toward her. "I don't want to talk anymore."

Joseph appeared in the doorway. Before she even had time to react, he lifted his gun and knocked Clive on the head. The man slid out of the chair and crumpled to the floor, lying on his side with the gun inches from his fingers.

Joy and relief flooded through her. He put a finger over his lips to indicate she needed to be quiet. She wanted to hug him, to feel the safety of being in his arms. She couldn't stop those feelings.

He pulled a knife out of his back pocket and untied the ropes that bound her.

He signaled for her to follow. As she stepped over Clive, who lay unconscious on the floor, she said a quick prayer for him.

They hurried out of the room and into a sort of hallway that opened into the engine room. Two men, one of them piloting the boat, stood with their backs to them. So there were four men on board.

"Heathen wants to have a big meeting the weekend of the boat show. He says it will provide good cover for us," said the man behind the wheel of the boat.

Crouching low, Joseph stopped at the ladder. Sierra pressed close to him on the other side of the doorway. He seemed to have halted to listen to the conversation.

"He's the boss. I think being spotted made him nervous," said the man standing beside the pilot.

Even from the back, she recognized the muscular man who had planted the bomb in the shop. The reference to the boss, the one they called Heathen, must be the man she'd seen in the forest. Heathen had to be some sort of code name. No one would name their kid that.

"In another ten minutes, that won't be an issue, will it?"

Both men laughed.

Sierra's throat went tight. She had been ten minutes away from death.

Joseph signaled for her to go up the ladder.

With Joseph right behind her, she hurried up the rungs and out onto the deck.

Joseph grabbed her hand and led her toward a dinghy that she hadn't noticed.

They hurried past a man who lay motionless on his stomach. Joseph must have disabled him. That was what the noise had been about earlier.

He released the dinghy. Before it even landed in the water, he grabbed Sierra's hand. "Hurry."

Jumping into the smaller boat while the bigger boat was moving was not a precision act. They both landed outside the boat and swam toward it. The larger boat sped away. Both of them grabbed an oar and rowed in the opposite direction of the boat.

The bigger boat slowed and then began to turn in a wide arc. Their escape had been discovered. Sierra glanced all around at the expansive dark water. She still couldn't see the shore anywhere.

They'd be an easy target if they stayed in the boat.

The larger boat had turned completely around and was headed back toward them.

It looked like her life had been extended by only minutes, and now Joseph would die, too.

THIRTEEN

As the larger boat drew nearer, Joseph assessed their options. The list was short. "Get out of the boat."

"But there's no place to swim to."

"Do it, Sierra. Stay underwater as much as possible."

He heard a splash as she slid off the side of the dinghy. He got into the water, as well, but stayed close to the boat, intending to use it as a shield. The cold water suctioned around his lower body. He pulled out the gun Cindy had given him.

He dipped down below the rim of the dinghy, listening to the sound of the approaching boat. A light shone across the top of the dinghy. He lifted his head just above the rim of the boat.

Three of the four men were on deck, walking the length of the boat. One of them had a searchlight.

Once he'd fired off a round, he'd give himself away. He had to make the shot count. The larger boat inched closer.

His finger rested on the trigger. Water bombarded him as he clung to the boat. His hand moved up and down with the waves. A solid shot was not going to be easy. He steadied himself and stared down the gun sight. Aiming for the larger man, his finger pressed the trigger. He squeezed off a round.

One of the men on deck crumpled to the deck. In the chaos that followed with the other two men in a panic, he was able to get off another shot. He heard a yelp. He must have at least nicked one of them.

One of the men had retrieved a rifle and aimed it toward the dinghy. Joseph tossed the gun in the dinghy and dipped underwater. Holding on to it would slow him down, and taking it underwater might render it useless.

Staying underwater, he swam away from the dinghy. He resurfaced some distance from the smaller boat. Now there was only one man on deck, who paced, holding the rifle. The boat trolled up and down a short distance, getting closer to him.

He dipped back under the cold water and kept swimming. He'd seen no sign of Sierra. He had to trust that she had put some distance between herself and the men on the boat.

When he could hold his breath no longer, he bobbed to the surface. The boat continued to troll the water but had gotten farther away. He swam in the opposite direction, coming to the surface to get his breath and then going back under. Each time he looked around for Sierra, but didn't see her.

He swam for what felt like a half hour, but it had to be less. His body was fatiguing from the exertion, and his muscles cramped from the cold. He stopped and treaded water.

The lights of the boat twinkled far in the distance, the sound of the engine barely discernable. His heart squeezed tight. Still no sign of Sierra.

A light-colored object floated on the water. He swam toward it. A wide piece of lumber. He crawled onto it and pulled his knees up to his chest. Floating on his makeshift boat would at least allow him to rest. The nighttime temperatures and his soaking clothes chilled him to the bone. Where was Sierra?

He hadn't had time to process the conversation they'd overheard on the boat. Heathen must be a code name, and he must be very important in the drug network. Maybe he was the man Sierra had seen in the woods. In any case, something important was going to happen at the boat show.

He heard a splash behind him. Sierra held on to the edge of the thick plank.

"Come here often?" She wiped water from her face.

"What's a beautiful dame like you doing in a joint like this?" He held his hand out for her to get on the board as the tightness in his chest melted away. At least she'd made it.

She sat beside him, their shoulders touching. She, too, was shivering. She pointed off in the distance, where there was a variation in the shadows. "I think that's the shoreline."

"Good, we can't stay in this water much longer."

They both slipped back into the water, using the wood as a paddleboard to conserve energy. The shoreline became more distinct as they drew nearer. He welcomed the sound of the waves hitting the beach.

The moment his feet touched solid ground, he let go of the plank and walked the remaining distance to land. Water dripped off him. The trees grew close to the shoreline.

Sierra wrapped her arms around herself in an effort to keep warm. They had no shelter and no way to build a fire.

"Do you know where we're at?"

She shook her head. "This is really remote.

I've never been to this part of the lake. If we could get through the thick of the trees, there might be some landmarks that would help me figure out which way leads back to Scenic View."

"I think we're miles from anywhere." He shifted his weight glancing around. "It's kind of dark."

They walked deeper into the evergreen forest. "Fine by me. I need to rest anyway." Sierra collapsed on the ground and pressed her back against a tree. The waver in her voice told him she wouldn't be able to walk very far.

With his pocketknife, he cut off some evergreen boughs. Though it was warm enough that hypothermia was not a danger, they were both shivering. He tossed the boughs toward her. "It's not a blanket, but it will help." There was no point in stumbling around in the dark in a place neither of them were familiar with. They'd only wear themselves out more. Sleep was the best thing for them right now.

Sierra pulled the boughs around her.

He sat beside her. "I can wrap my arm around you, if that's all right. We can warm each other up."

She nodded. He gathered her into his arms. She grabbed more of the boughs and placed them on his back and shoulders as he drew his legs up. She rested her head against his shoulder. Her wet hair touched the underside of his chin.

She trembled in his arms. It took him a moment to realize she was sobbing.

"Hey, it's not so bad. We'll be able to figure out where we are as soon as we have some light."

"It's not that." She nestled a little deeper against his chest. "It's just… I almost died back there. It was minutes away. If you hadn't shown up, I would have."

He held her a little tighter. "That's what we do. We have each other's back."

Gradually, she stopped shaking from crying and grew still. Though he was also cold and tired, it felt good to hold her.

His hand touched her damp hair with a featherlight touch. He felt himself pulled between worlds. The one that was filled with danger and a sense of purpose, and the one that nourished his soul, here in the darkness holding Sierra.

A tight twisting sensation invaded his chest cavity. His whole identity was wrapped up in being an agent. He couldn't give it up, could he? This feeling in his chest could only be one thing…heartbreak.

He jerked free from the embrace and rose to

his feet, pacing. "So we should probably take shifts and keep watch through the night. I'll take first shift and wake you in a few hours. You can wake me at first light."

"Okay," she said. Her voice sounded far away as though she were deep in thought.

The sun warmed Sierra's skin as it snuck through the tree canopy. They'd made it through the night. Joseph lay on the ground still asleep. He looked cute with his eyes closed and his long hair flopping over his cheek.

Pain sliced through her heart. He'd pulled away from their hug last night. Fine, she was attracted to him. Fine, she felt safe with him. He'd made it clear there wasn't going to be anything between them. They were allies fighting the same war on different fronts. That was all it was, and all it would ever be.

Joseph's eyes opened and he sat up with a start, as though some inner terror had alerted him.

"Bad dreams?"

He ran his hands through his shaggy hair, then placed his arms on his knees. "Something like that."

His gaze rested on her. His stiff, hypervigilant posture relaxed a bit. "Hey, good morning."

When he looked at her like that, her heart beat

a little faster. "Looks like we made it through the night."

Her stomach growled. She pushed herself to her feet. They were surrounded by forest. "Let's hike to an open spot and see if we can get our bearings as to which direction is home."

She reached out a hand to help him up. He rose to his feet, holding on to her hand. Again, she felt a charge of electricity between them as his palm pressed against hers.

He let go of her hand and touched his shirt. "Still damp."

"The sun should dry our clothes out the rest of the way."

"Maybe the smart thing to do would be to stay close to the shoreline," he said.

"It could be miles before we run into anything or anyone. If we get out of these trees, I would have a better idea of where we're at."

He furrowed his forehead as his mouth formed a straight line.

Her voice had a bit of an edge to it. She realized she wasn't really fighting about what they should do next, but was still reeling from the hurt of him not returning her affection at the office.

She softened her words. "Then maybe we can head back toward the lake if I don't see a clear direction out or signs of a cabin or camp or something."

Joseph shrugged. "You know this area better than I do."

They tromped through the trees. She heard the sound of a trickling stream and followed it.

They both kneeled and drank from their cupped hands. Her belly felt hollow.

She rose to her feet after a few more gulps of water and placed her palm on her growly stomach. "Right now, I'm dreaming of scampi fried in butter and garlic and a big salad."

Joseph offered her a faint smile. "Steak and fries for me, with a big milkshake."

She started walking. "And for dessert, apple crisp." She glanced over her shoulder, appreciating the amused look on his face.

"This Southern boy would take some peach pie, thank you very much."

She laughed, feeling a spring return to her step as they entered a wide meadow.

The sound of a small plane engine filled the sky around them. They both tilted their heads, searching the clear blue above them.

"A search plane, do you think?"

"Yeah, it's a possibility. Cindy might have called in search and rescue when we didn't make contact after a few hours."

The plane dropped dramatically in elevation as it swept over them. Sierra waved her arms.

The plane flew out some distance before turning.

"That doesn't look like a search and rescue plane." He reached out and grabbed her arm. "And wouldn't they send a chopper out so they could land and pick us up?" Fear permeated Joseph's voice.

The plane loomed toward them, dipping even lower. Terror seized her heart. There were no markings on the plane to indicate it was search and rescue. The plane was the type that could land on the water. It dipped down even lower as it flew toward the lake.

"It could just be a private citizen who spotted us. I don't want to risk missing out on a rescue," she said.

They could hear the sound of the plane engine sputtering to a stop as it landed on the water.

Joseph's hand slipped into hers. "Let's circle around and see who gets out of that plane."

Sierra took in a prayer-filled breath.

Please, God, let this be someone who can help us.

They sprinted through the trees down to the shoreline. The plane had landed about twenty yards up from where they were. Using the brush for cover, they watched as an inflatable boat was tossed onto the lake. Two men jumped out, both of them holding rifles.

Sierra's pulse pounded in her ears.

So that was it. They were about to be hunted like animals.

FOURTEEN

Joseph grabbed Sierra's hand. They headed toward the thick of the forest. Behind them, the plane engine roared back to life. So they would be hunted on the ground and in the air. No doubt, the spotter on the plane would be able to communicate with the two men with rifles as to where he and Sierra were running.

As long as they had the trees for cover, the plane wouldn't be able to see them as easily. He was plagued by the notion that he had valuable intel about the big meeting to take place at the boat show and no way to get that information to anyone who could make a difference.

They had to get out of this forest alive.

It was only a matter of minutes before they heard the men with rifles moving through the forest, closing in on them. The plane flew over again.

He glanced up at the canopy of trees. Only a little sunlight snuck through. Noises off to the side alerted him to how close one of the men was getting.

He grabbed Sierra and pulled her toward some brush, where they crouched. He was able to catch flashes of movement through the foliage. The man with the rifle ran past them, then slowed his steps, looking around. In addition to the rifle, he had a handgun in a holster on his belt.

These men had come armed to the teeth to ensure that he and Sierra didn't get of there alive. The other man came through the trees. The two men spoke in low tones before one of them pointed to the east. The second man took off running deeper into the forest, away from the shoreline.

The first man continued to search the area where he and Sierra were hiding. It was just a matter of time before he got close enough to see them. But if they ran, they would be spotted for sure. Joseph's heart pounded as sweat trickled past his temple. The first man must have sensed that they were close because he kept circling the area, taking a step and then looking around. Like a hunter trying to track a deer.

The plane engine sputtered and hummed in the distance, flying over them in the opposite direction.

The assassin loomed closer to them. They had only one option that seemed viable.

Joseph leaned close to Sierra ear. "It's two against one."

She nodded. "I'll distract. You jump him."

He hated the plan. It put Sierra in danger. But it was their only option.

She jumped up and raced toward a cluster of trees. Though she would not be seen, the noise should be enough to send the hunter in her direction.

The hunter ran past the bush where Joseph waited. Joseph leaped through the air, landing on the man's back and taking him to the ground. The man dropped his rifle but managed to flip over and throw Joseph off.

The man reached for his handgun, but Joseph landed a blow to his jaw that stunned him. The man blinked as his eyes watered from the pain. This man was not one of the guys they had dealt with previously.

Joseph lifted his hand to hit the man again. The man blocked the shot and threw Joseph on the ground, hard enough that it knocked the wind out of Joseph. This assassin was a big man, strong and clearly had some martial arts training.

In the second it took Joseph to recover from landing on his back, the man pulled the gun and aimed it at Joseph, preparing to shoot.

Sierra came up behind the man, lifted a thick

stick she had picked up and hit him on the side of the head. The man stumbled backward but remained upright. Joseph landed a blow to the man's stomach that doubled him over. Sierra hit the man again. This time he fell to the ground.

"Good teamwork." Joseph kneeled beside the assassin to check for a pulse and grab the man's phone. Not only was the phone evidence, but it would allow him to call Cindy and alert her of their position once they threw off the other pursuers.

Sierra picked up the gun and handed it to Joseph.

The plane flew over them again. They were in a clearing and easy enough to spot.

"That other guy is going to know to come back this way. Let's get some distance between us so we can find a hiding place and I can phone for some help."

They ran through the forest in a zigzag pattern. The sound of the lake breaking on the shore reached his ears. He directed them back deeper into the forest.

As the trees thinned, he looked over his shoulder and caught the glint of metal that must have been the sun reflecting off the other man's rifle. The second assassin was gaining on them. Both the assassins had been dressed in camo, which made it hard to gauge how close they were. They weren't going to outrun the guy.

They needed to find a hiding place. Even as his feet pounded the ground, he scanned the area around them, hoping to spot a place that would conceal them.

Both of them sprinted, jumping over logs and pushing branches out of the way. When he craned his neck, he could no longer see any movement that looked human. The only sound he heard was the breeze blowing through the higher branches, making them creak.

Sierra slowed her pace. Glancing all around and breathing heavily, she whispered, "Did we lose him?"

The assassin moved silently through the forest and was hard to see. They couldn't take any chances.

Joseph tugged on her sleeve. "Let's keep going."

They ran for another twenty minutes until the forest ended and they came out into an open area that slanted uphill. The plane had not passed over them for some time. When he scanned the tree line, he saw no sign of the assassin, no movement.

The land grew rockier, and he heard the sound of a waterfall.

Sierra pointed toward a distant mountain

peak. "I know about where we are. We're west of Eclipse Falls."

Joseph pulled his phone out, still watching the trees, and dialed Cindy's number.

She picked up right away. "Yes?"

"It's Joseph. We don't have much time. We're west of Eclipse Falls."

"I'm glad you're alive. I alerted search and rescue, but they had no idea where to look. They shouldn't be long since they're already mobilized."

"We'll try to stay in the area, but we're being pursued."

"Gotcha," said Cindy.

Sierra touched Joseph's hand to get his attention. "Tell her we'll head toward the falls," said Sierra. "If we climb to the top, we'll be able to see the guy with the rifle coming. Plus, a chopper can land above the falls pretty easily. They can spot us from the air."

Joseph relayed the additional information before clicking off the phone.

Sierra took off at an intense run, and he fell in beside her.

When he looked over his shoulder, he saw movement along the tree line they had just come from.

They slipped into the forest on the other side

of the open area. He had to assume the assassin was still right on their tail.

Sierra's legs felt like they were on fire. Her muscles screamed from the exertion of climbing uphill. Only the sound of the falls growing louder gave her the incentive to keep going.

The trees thinned and the ground became rockier. They followed the trail upward. The noise of water falling and crashing against rock seemed to surround them. They rounded a curve in the trail and the waterfall came into view.

Sierra pointed off to the side. "There's a place there where you can climb around and get to the top."

"It looks steep."

"We used to climb it on a dare when I was a teenager." She headed toward the side of the waterfall, taking the time to scan the forest below her. Had they managed to throw the guy off, or was he hidden somewhere down there, looking for the opportunity to line up a shot?

She traversed the boulders with the roar of the waterfall in her ears. They were close enough that water sprayed them. Some of the rocks and ground were unstable. She chose her path carefully. Joseph followed behind, taking the same path she had.

A rifle shot pinged through the air just in

front of her. Heart pounding, she slipped behind a large rock, pulling herself into a ball. Down below, Joseph lay on his stomach. She peered above the rock but could not see the assassin anywhere. He could be behind one of the boulders or still hidden in the forest.

She tried to take in a deep breath to shake off the terror that permeated her awareness. They might die out here.

Though he remained low to the ground, Joseph had started to crawl upward again. She couldn't stay here forever. She climbed upward.

In the distance, she heard the sound of a helicopter.

When she looked down below, she saw a man at the edge of the trees.

Another shot resounded through the air. Joseph groaned.

She glanced over at him. Blood seeped out from beneath his hand where he pressed it against his shoulder. He'd been shot.

She cried out to him.

"I'm all right."

The anguish in his voice told her he was lying.

The *whop, whop, whop* of the helicopter blades grew louder. She worked her way over to him.

"Come on, we can make it." She lifted him to his feet, and they ran the remaining distance up to the plateau where the chopper hovered. The rush of the waterfall and the mechanical hum of the helicopter engulfed her.

The assassin had receded back into the trees. The chopper continued to angle from side to side, as if it was trying to land.

Joseph stumbled. She wrapped her arm around his waist in an effort to support him.

The chopper hovered a few feet above the ground. A man appeared in the opening of the helicopter, holding out his arms to indicate he would help lift them to safety.

Joseph bent over at the waist from the pain. He straightened and reached up.

The man dragged Joseph into the helicopter. He groaned in pain as he was pulled in. She glanced down the steep incline. No sign of the assassin. Either he didn't want to risk being seen, or taking out the search and rescue crew was more collateral damage than even he could handle.

The rescuer reached down for Sierra and pulled her in. An EMT was already leaning over Joseph, taking his vitals and tearing away shirt fabric to examine the bullet wound.

All the color had drained from Joseph's face. She scooted toward him as the chopper rose in the air. He held out his uninjured arm to her. She put her hand in his.

She turned toward the EMT. "How is he?"

"The bullet tore through muscle. No vital organs since it's a shoulder wound, but he's losing a lot of blood. We need to get him to a hospital and quick."

Joseph closed his eyes. Sierra squeezed his hand, and he squeezed back.

The flight back into town seemed to take forever. She watched the landscape clip by below, forest, lake and mountains. Finally, the outskirts of Scenic View—scattered farmhouses and fields of cattle—came into view.

She took in a breath when she saw the hospital, which towered over the surrounding buildings. The chopper landed on the roof, where a crew was waiting to load Joseph onto a stretcher.

She followed behind. Once inside the hospital, Joseph was stabilized in the ER and then whisked into surgery, which was on another floor. Sierra collapsed on a hard plastic chair. She sat for a long time, staring at the wall.

She had no idea how much time had passed when a nurse touched her on the shoulder.

She startled, suddenly aware of her environment. "Is he going to be okay?"

"He's still in surgery. Are you his wife?"

"No, I'm his…girlfriend."

"You'll want to notify his family." She handed her the phone Joseph had taken off the assassin.

"Yes, of course." She stared at the phone. Not only did she not know Joseph's family, notifying them might risk his cover being blown. Cindy's number came up as the last number called. He could at least have a colleague around when he woke up.

She phoned Cindy's number and let her know what the situation was. Cindy promised to come right over.

She sat in the chair, watching the comings and goings in the ER. Still unable to shake her anxiety, she rose to her feet. The ER was set up in a square, with a wide corridor between rooms on the perimeter and an administration desk in the center. She paced several laps through the ER, still gripping the phone in her hand.

She walked past a room where a distraught-looking man stood with his arms crossed over his chest while a child wailed inside the room. What a horrible thing, to have to live through seeing your child in pain.

The curtain was only half-drawn on a room where an older woman sat beside a gray-haired man in a bed.

Finally, she walked past a room where several cops stood while a man who clearly had overdone it with drugs or alcohol hollered about how everyone had taken advantage of him.

The phone buzzed. A text had come in.

Thinking it might hold information that would help Joseph with his investigation, she clicked on it.

We're watching you, Sierra.

Her throat constricted as she gripped the phone and looked around the ER. One of the cops outside the intoxicated man's door held his phone. She remembered what Joseph had said about the DEA's suspicions that someone in the police department was tipping the drug dealers off.

The police officer returned his attention to his phone. A man in a suit stood off in a corner. He held a phone in his hand, as well. There was something sinister about his grin when he noticed Sierra looking at him. Maybe it was just her paranoia. With her heart still racing, she looked away and then stared down at the phone again.

A chill skittered across her nerves like a thousand tiny spider legs.

"Sierra." A hand touched her shoulder, and she jumped. Cindy stood behind her. "Hey, I didn't mean to startle you."

"It's okay." She handed Cindy the phone. "Joseph wanted this to be looked at for evidence.

A threatening text directed at me just came in on it."

Cindy gathered Sierra in her arms. "That must have been so scary."

Sierra appreciated Cindy's compassion, but it did nothing to allay her fears.

A nurse came toward them. "Joseph is out of surgery. He'll be in recovery in just a little bit."

Sierra breathed a sigh of relief for Joseph. As she followed Cindy back toward the waiting room, she was grateful to have some measure of protection. But it was very apparent that the reach of this drug network and the man behind it, the one they called Heathen, could get to her almost anywhere.

FIFTEEN

Sierra, with her bright smile, stepped into Joseph's hospital room. "So, you ready to go home?" Her light blue sundress matched her eyes. Her dark hair was pulled up into a pony-tail. The word *radiant* came into his head when he looked at her.

The memory of watching over her while she slept in the forest still played in the corners of his mind.

After two days, Joseph had had enough of hospitals. He was glad to be checking out and getting back to work, even if it was in a limited capacity. The soreness from the bullet wound was intense enough that he couldn't lift his arm above his head.

"Where's Cindy? She's supposed to stay with you at all times." He hated that he couldn't be the one to protect her.

"Relax, she just stopped to go to the little

girls' room. She's been great. She even helped me with youth group last night."

Joseph was seated in a chair by the window. He was already dressed and beyond ready to leave this place. He had a limited range of motion in his shoulder, but the doctor had assured him he'd be back to normal in a month to six weeks—a diagnosis he wasn't happy with. He wasn't about to quit his undercover work.

The time in the hospital had allowed him to touch bases with his handler. They both agreed that surveillance of the boat show might help flush out the man Sierra had seen in the woods. The problem was, Sierra was the only one who knew what he looked like. He didn't feel good about putting her in the line of fire, even if he had all kinds of backup. The DEA had come up with a plan that he thought might work and would keep Sierra safe, if she was open to it.

Sierra walked over to the window and stared out at the sculpture garden. The view out his window had been the one nice thing about being in the hospital. "What was the news you took on the phone about the assassin? Was it helpful in any way?"

He'd seen the text threat directed at Sierra, and he was sure that was on her mind. Even if she didn't mention it outright, he detected the note of fear in her voice.

"Forensics is still going through it. There were some fingerprints on it. Most of the numbers, though, were from disposable phones."

"Kind of a dead end, then. The boat show might be the only way we'll ever catch the man I saw."

He appreciated that she wanted to help. Despite being afraid, she was willing to put herself in danger. "You have been through a lot."

"I want to see this thing to the end. I want that man to go to jail. I want the kids I care about to have a shot at a decent life."

"Sierra, I think we have a plan for you to help us ID the guy you saw without having to be out in the open."

She crossed her arms over her chest and narrowed her eyes at him. "How else will you catch him?"

"The DEA is sending in tons of surveillance. We know who some of his associates are, thanks to your IDs. We have access to databases filled with photographs of past surveillance that we can cross-reference and match past photos with the people at the boat show. We have a drone."

"None of that is as good as me seeing the guy."

"Exactly. So what the DEA is proposing is having you in a secure location—probably a hotel room in the resort—where you can watch the surveillance footage as it comes in." He turned slightly and winced at the pain. "Since I'm not a hundred percent, I'll stay with you, along with a DEA tech guy. We can't post a guard outside the door, as that would draw attention."

She stared at him for a long moment. "That sounds really safe, and that way we could cover a lot more ground."

"Good, then. We might be able to wrap this investigation up." With some effort, he leaned forward to get out of his chair.

"Yes indeed, and then you will be on to the next thing, right?" The temperature in the room seemed to drop several degrees.

He detected a note of hurt in her voice. "It's what I do, Sierra." They had to be realistic here.

She turned away from him and pointed toward a bag with the hospital logo on it. "Do you want me to carry your stuff out?"

He'd clearly upset her, thus the quick change in subject. "I can handle it. My right arm still works just fine. I'm not a baby." His voice had a little bit of an edge to it, too.

Cindy stood in the doorway holding a can of soda. "Got thirsty. Couldn't find the coffee. You two ready?"

Cindy drove Joseph back to his shop, which

Jake had pretty much been running for the last two days.

Joseph worked in the shop for the next couple of days while the plans for the surveillance were being put into place. Because lots of out-of-towners showed up for the boat show, the flood of extra agents would not be noticed.

At four o'clock, Joseph left Jake in charge of the shop and headed out to pick up Sierra and Cindy. Though there was already some preliminary activity, the plan was to have Sierra moved into the hotel room the night before the boat show officially started. It was apparent that the drug network had eyes everywhere. Sierra was less likely to be noticed if she was in place before all the hubbub started.

Joseph drove to Sierra's house. As he parked on the street outside it, he glanced around. Her place might be under watch. The lots in this neighborhood were big. Though some distance away, Sierra's grain silo house was next to a trailer with a front yard filled with lawnmowers that the man apparently repaired and sold. A strange car would be easily noticed.

Sierra and Cindy emerged and got into the car. Cindy got behind the wheel. Sierra carried a large tote.

With the knowledge that Sierra's house might be under surveillance, they'd come up with a plan to throw off any tail. They drove to a downtown department store, where they would purchase clothes that were out of character for both of them, along with hats that would cover their faces. Before they got out of the car, she opened her big tote and handed him a bag that she had stored in there.

"Good luck, you two." Cindy kept the car running. "We'll catch up with you back at the hotel."

They entered the department store separately.

Joseph felt a knot of tension form at the back of his neck as he selected clothes from a clearance rack. He peered over the rack to see Sierra grabbing something pink. She met his gaze before disappearing into the women's dressing room.

He hurried to his dressing room, changing quickly and stuffing his old clothes in the tote. He stepped back into the store to pay for his purchases. He pushed the price tags across the counter and whispered to the clerk so as not to draw attention. "I'll be wearing the outfit." He didn't see Sierra anywhere. His throat went tight. He had to trust in the plan.

A car that agents had left for them earlier was parked on a side street. He stepped out with the late-day sun still beating down on him. He pulled the keys from his pocket and stood on the sidewalk, watching the doors. His heartbeat drummed in his ears.

"You look like you're about ready for a board meeting."

He jumped at the sound of Sierra's voice. He stared down at the dress pants and button-down shirt he'd chosen. He'd also purchased a golf cap that concealed part of his face.

Her blue eyes twinkled. She wore a bohemian-style maxidress in pink florals and a large floppy hat.

"You look like you're on your way to the hippie commune," he said.

"We don't exactly match," she said. "I mean, we don't look like…a couple that would be together."

He hurried around the car to open the door for her. "Sometimes opposites attract."

She got into the car and looked up at him. "It's all just a big fiction, anyway, right?"

The tone of her voice tugged at his heart. He didn't have a response to the hurt he picked up on. He'd been brisk with her, even cold, though she deserved nothing but kindness. "I'll always count you as a friend, an ally." More than anything, he wanted to take her pain away.

Warmth came into her eyes. "That's something."

They drove to the resort, parked and walked

toward the hotel. The place already looked busier than usual. More boats were out on the water and at the dock. A rock band played on the grassy area beside the hotel entrance. There was a planned boat race, as well as numerous boats that would be on display inside and outside the hotel. Merchandisers had set up kiosks outside.

They entered the hotel.

"We're on the seventh floor." Joseph pointed toward the elevator that was on the other side of the marbled corridor. The door slid open. A broad-shouldered man stepped out, and Joseph recognized him instantly—the assassin whose phone he had taken after knocking him out.

"They're here already," said Joseph.

Joseph grabbed Sierra and kissed her, so their faces would be hidden beneath her hat. The instant his lips touched hers and he felt her respond, he knew he wasn't pretending.

He couldn't lie to himself anymore. He loved her.

When he thought enough time had passed for the assassin to walk past them, he pulled free of the kiss. His muscles felt electrified, and his heart raced.

Sierra's eyes searched his.

His cheeks warmed.

"I saw him, too," she said. She took a step

back. Her voice held no emotion. She could have been talking about the price of tea in China.

She was all business. He'd spurned her enough that she had probably closed her heart to him. He loved her, but he'd figured it out too late.

Joseph turned three quarters of a circle, searching every section of the open area of the resort. The assassin must have gone down one of the side corridors where the smaller shops were. Joseph looked through the big floor-to-ceiling glass walls that provided a view of the marina.

Or the man had stepped outside.

He turned to face Sierra. The edges of her mouth twitched, but her eyes revealed nothing.

His heartbeat still hadn't returned to normal. Just when she seemed to be accepting that he couldn't get involved, he was realizing that leaving her would be the hardest thing he ever did.

Sierra thought her knees would buckle and she'd fall on the marble floor. Joseph's kiss had turned her inside out and upside down. But he'd made it clear there could be nothing between them, so she wasn't about to be vulnerable with him. She'd worn her heart on her sleeve just a little too readily.

Though she'd felt an attraction to him even

before he was shot, seeing him come near death had caused something to shift for her. She pictured a life without him, and the heartache over that was like a wave that threatened to pull her under, deprive her of oxygen.

"Maybe we should take the stairs." Joseph leaned close and spoke in low tones. His palm cupped her elbow. "Safer, I think."

The warmth of his touch sent a new wave of sadness through her. To all the world, they looked like a couple who had come to enjoy the boat show.

"Hey, Miss M."

Sierra whirled around as Ginny came toward her.

"Miss M! Sierra!" Ginny yelled her name again.

Joseph glanced around, clearly nervous. "Say your hellos and let's get out of here. We don't need to be out in the open any longer. And the kid just let everyone know who you are."

Ginny ran up to her, and she hugged the teenager.

"What are you doing here?" She looked at Joseph. "I heard you were with the skateboard shop guy."

The words cut like a knife. "Ginny, I'm so sorry, but we are in a little bit of a hurry." She squeezed Ginny's hand. "I promise to catch up with you at group next week."

Ginny's expression clouded with disappointment. "Sure." Or maybe the pinched features were confusion.

Her reaction to Ginny was very out of character. Any time she saw one of her kids, she made it a point to plant her feet and listen to what they had to say.

Joseph all but pulled her toward the stairwell. His hand gripped hers like iron. He pushed open the stairwell doors. "You go in front." As he glanced over his shoulder at the open area, he touched inside his jacket where his gun was. She was grateful his shooting hand wasn't connected to the injured shoulder.

They hurried up the first three flights, not encountering anyone. Both of them slowed down a little.

Joseph said, "You're probably tired of all this exercise, but it would be easier to deal with an attacker on the stairs. I just didn't want to get trapped in an elevator, knowing that some of the henchmen are already at the hotel."

As they climbed the stairs, an unnamed tension coiled around her. The kiss had probably meant nothing to him, just part of the job.

They stepped out onto the seventh floor. Joseph led them down the hall.

They passed a woman coming toward them in a cocktail dress and heels. Sierra made eye contact, then looked away, realizing that was probably a bad idea. The woman looked vaguely familiar, she thought as she headed toward the elevator.

Joseph swiped his card in front of door 726. A man of about twenty got off the elevator and headed up the hallway toward them, walking with a purpose. The intensity of the man's gait made Sierra's heart flutter. She stared at the floor and pressed a little closer to Joseph. The man walked past.

Joseph stepped to one side so she could enter the room first. Inside, several monitors had already been set up. A bald man wearing glasses bustled around the room, unwinding extension cords.

"You made it." Though the man had to be at least forty, he was as lean and athletic as Joseph.

"Sierra, this is Agent Mike Alvarez." Joseph gave the other agent a friendly slug in the shoulder. "Don't let the nerdiness fool you. He's a black belt and a better shot than me, and he's in charge of this surveillance operation."

Sierra held out her hand to Agent Alvarez.

"So, what do I do now?"

Joseph hurried over to the sliding glass door that led to a balcony. He drew the curtains shut, making the room even dimmer and more depressing. "You wait. You brought a book, right?"

Joseph and Mike engaged in shoptalk as they set up the equipment. Sierra pulled her book from the tote. The hotel room was a suite with a separate sleeping area. She wandered into the bedroom and plunked down on the bed.

The boat show didn't start until tomorrow at ten. She stared at her book and then the television. The next sixteen or so hours were going to be an exercise in entertaining herself with very little to work with. Joseph had made it clear she couldn't even look out the window. A heaviness fell on her that was brought on by more than just the impending boredom.

She could hear Joseph and Mike laughing and joking, reliving some case they had worked together. She was separate from his world now.

She switched out of the dress and back into her more comfortable capris and blouse. Then she lay on the bed, resting her head on the pillow and staring at the ceiling. She'd brought other things to entertain herself, as well—a journal, a travel watercolor kit. Right now, in this moment, though, it all seemed quite pointless.

She closed her eyes. The fog of sleep drifted across her brain. Was it sadness or exhaustion that made her want to sleep? She couldn't say.

She shifted to her side and pulled the pillow out from underneath the cover, then closed her eyes as her muscles relaxed.

When she awoke, there was no noise in the next room. She checked the bedside clock. She'd been asleep for less than two hours. She entered the other room, where Joseph was kneeling behind a monitor adjusting something on the back of it.

"Hey, Sleeping Beauty." He lifted his head above the monitor. His smile lit up the room.

"You seem happy," she said.

All but one of the monitors showed some part of the marina, as well as the corridors of the resort.

He came out from behind the bank of monitors and crossed his arms. "It's just good to be working with Mike again. We've done quite a few assignments together."

She hadn't thought of it until now, but undercover work must be lonely. He couldn't reveal his true self to many people. "Where is Mike, anyway?"

"There was something wrong with one of the cameras we set up. He went out to see if he could fix it."

She nodded, watching the monitors. It must be dinnertime. The restaurants in the resorts bustled with activity. Several of them had a line of people waiting to be seated.

"I ordered some room service. It should be here shortly. When the guy knocks, you can go into the other room. Just as a precaution."

She studied the monitors. There was some sort of ceremony taking place on the green with the police officers. There were seven men and one woman standing at attention in uniform, as well as a woman dressed in slacks and a blouse. Her attention was drawn to a camera that covered the area where vendors were showing off boat-related merchandise. She recognized some of the local companies, but several were businesses she had never heard of—a company that sold outboard motors, and another called Blue Devil, with boat cleaning products.

There was a knock on the door. "Room service."

Joseph looked at her and nodded. She retreated to the bedroom and listened to the friendly exchange between Joseph and the room service woman.

As the images she had just seen on the monitors flashed through her brain, something clicked into place. The woman she had seen in the cocktail dress earlier on this floor was the same woman standing beside the uniformed officer on the monitor. She was the dispatcher for

the police department. Sierra had seen her at
fund-raisers. She wasn't sure why the change
in clothing or what it meant. It just seemed odd.

She heard Joseph thank the room service
woman. She waited for the sound of the door
clicking shut.

And then a crashing noise, something being
banged around, reached her ears. At first, she
thought maybe the monitors had fallen over.
She hurried to the doorway in time to see Joseph wrestling with the broad-shouldered man
they'd seen earlier.

She shot a glance toward the monitors, where
something caught her eye. And suddenly everything clicked into place. She knew who Heathen was.

A second man pressed a gun against her back.
"You're coming with me."

SIXTEEN

The assassin had gotten the upper hand in his fight with Joseph and now rested his knees on Joseph's chest. He lifted his arm to land a blow across Joseph's face. He blocked the hit. The two men had come in through the balcony. They must have climbed over or down from another room.

In his peripheral vision, he saw movement—Sierra being escorted out of the room and the door closing. He was helpless to save her.

Something hit his head. Black dots filled his field of vision until he saw only a pinhole view of the hotel room. He felt the weight of the man on him lift just as his world went black…

He came to with Mike shaking him. "What happened? Where is Sierra?"

Joseph shook his head. Pain radiated through his injured shoulder where the man had punched him.

How had they found out where Sierra was?

The two men had slipped in so quietly and quickly, the room service attendant hadn't even been alarmed enough to come back or alert anyone. The attendant must have been far enough down the hallway not to hear the scuffle.

Mike repeated his question. "Where is Sierra?"

He barely uttered the words. "They took her." He felt like his whole world had been torn to pieces. He could no longer picture life without Sierra. Whatever it took he would get her back.

Mike jumped to his feet. "How long ago?"

Joseph was still having a hard time processing what had happened, partly because of the blow to his head but also because knowing he had let Sierra down made him angry at himself. He looked at the clock on the wall. "Five minutes, maybe ten." He didn't remember the exact time of the attack. It had been around six, the dinner hour.

"The place is crawling with agents. We'll find her."

Still a bit wobbly, Joseph rose to his feet while Mike got on the phone and alerted other agents as to what had happened.

Mike clamped his hand on Joseph's shoulder. "You watch the monitors. Radio in if you see anything."

"I want to help find her."

Mike pointed at the monitors. "You will be helping. You're still not a hundred percent with that injury and you were just hit in the head."

"I know what a concussion feels like. My head is fine," said Joseph.

"Stay here, that's an order."

Mike was his superior. As angry as it made him, he couldn't argue with an order. He plunked down in the chair and studied the monitors. He recognized his fellow agents moving toward the resort exits. Two others searched the marina.

Helplessness enveloped him like a shroud. His hand curled into a fist as he clenched his jaw. How could he let this happen? An image of Sierra with a gun shoved in her back flashed through his mind. He felt like he'd been punched in the stomach.

As though zooming in, his brain recalled the picture of Sierra just as she was pulled through the door, and his world went black. Her expression had changed when she glanced at the monitors. She'd seen something.

He glanced at the time on the monitors. Now it mattered very much if the attack had happened five or ten minutes ago. Ten minutes was enough time to get downstairs via the elevator and out onto the street. But if he had only been unconscious for five minutes, she might still be in the building. Her captors would either be looking for a quiet place to kill her, or a way out so they could take her to a place where they could do away with her without witnesses.

He suspected the latter. Disposing of a body without being noticed was harder than moving a living person to a secluded location.

He checked the monitors that showed the marina. No boats had left the dock. The green in front of the resort was teeming with activity, vendors and a display of the newest models of boats, along with a band setting up on the grandstand, where the police department had just completed some kind of ceremony.

Joseph repositioned himself in the chair, then erupted from it and paced, still watching the monitors. Doing nothing was not his forte. He was a man of action.

He watched the monitors and recognized one of the men in the main corridor of the resort, Baseball Hat man. He was by himself. Judging from the way he paced and stopped to look around, then spoke into his collar, he was probably feeding information to someone about what he saw or suspected.

The man behind all this had probably gotten the information that there was more than one agent in the area. The two men who had breached the room and taken Sierra would have made note of the monitors.

Joseph watched the monitor where Baseball Hat slipped off the screen. He made note of the agent watching the door close to where Baseball Hat had gone and phoned him.

"Tall guy. Baseball hat, blue jacket," Joseph said.

"I see him," said the other agent.

"That guy has been after Sierra and I for days. Take him in for questioning. He might know where Sierra is."

"I need an order before I can do that."

Tension knotted around Joseph's chest and made it hard to breathe. "The clock is ticking here on Sierra's life. Bring him up here and I'll question him."

There was silence on the other end of the line.

"I'm sure the drug network is aware of our presence by now. Sierra's life is at stake, and she is the only one who can ID the man we're after."

"I'll bring him up if you clear it with Alvarez."

"I'll take care of it." Feeling a sense of urgency, Joseph phoned Mike Alvarez. After he explained the situation, Alvarez gave him the all-clear to take Baseball Hat man in.

"We've got two agents knocking on all the hotel room doors, posing as hotel employees answering a call for an air conditioner to be fixed. If we get anyone even acting a little strange, we'll take the steps to search the room."

Joseph hung up the phone and watched the monitors. If the agent was apprehending their suspect, it was taking place off screen.

The helplessness Joseph felt was like a weight on his chest. Sierra's life hung in the balance.

A few minutes later, he heard a tapping on the door. He unlocked it and slid back the dead bolt. A rookie agent that Joseph knew by face but not name stood with Baseball Hat man.

"Bring him in. Restrain him."

Before the man was even sitting down and handcuffed, Joseph stepped toward him. "Where have they taken Sierra?"

The man offered him an expression devoid of emotion. "Sierra who?"

Joseph leaned toward the man so their faces were only inches apart. "You know good and well who I'm talking about."

"Not my department," said Baseball Hat man.

"Is she still in the hotel?"

The man's mouth twitched, and his eyes widened slightly.

He was trying not to give anything away, but even that little bit of body language suggested that Joseph was right. They hadn't gotten Sierra out yet.

Joseph's mood elevated. Sierra was probably still alive, but he knew the clock was ticking.

The closet where they had stuffed Sierra was dark and cramped. With her back pressed against one wall, she had to bend her legs so her feet pushed against the opposite wall. The men who took her had hastily tied her hands together in front of her and put a gag in her mouth. She could hear the sound of the men arguing in the room.

"Why can't we just take care of her here and now?" one of them said.

"And do what with the body?" replied the other. "This place is crawling with agents. We can't take that risk. I don't want to go back to prison."

"We can just off her and get out of here," said the first voice.

"You don't think they have worked-up profiles on all of us? You don't think they are watching the exits?" She heard footsteps pounding. One of the men was pacing. "This is the DEA we're talking about."

There was a long moment of silence.

"Why should we kill this woman for Heathen if he's not going to help us?"

"Heathen has our back. You know that."

Sierra knew who Heathen was. She'd seen

him on the monitor seconds before she was abducted. Beside the display for Blue Devil boat cleaning products, she'd watched as the dispatcher for the police department kissed the man Sierra had seen in the forest, the man codenamed Heathen. Blue Devil cleaning products must be some kind of front. The leak in the police department wasn't an officer. It was the dispatcher, who must be Heathen's girlfriend.

She tilted her head and prayed. She had valuable information that could blow this whole thing apart.

God, get me out of here.

She heard a knock on the door. Then footsteps pounding. A hotel employee explaining that they had gotten a call from room 612 that the air-conditioning was broken.

She was only one floor below where Joseph was.

"We didn't call about that," said the man who had abducted her.

"Oh," said the hotel employee. "The room number must have gotten written down wrong."

She couldn't call out with the gag in her mouth. She lifted her feet and pounded the wall.

She heard the door slam shut.

Had the hotel employee heard her? She had no way of knowing.

The closet door swung open. A hand grabbed

her collar at the back of her neck and yanked her up.

"What do you think you're doing?"

Her knees felt like they might buckle from the terror inside her. She managed to plant her feet.

One of the men was the man who had threated her in the skateboard shop—the muscular man with big teeth. She didn't recognize the other man. He had long, dark hair braided into a ponytail.

The phone of Ponytail man rang. He put it to his ear. "Yep…okay…three minutes…got it. We'll be there." He hung up and looked at Big Teeth. "There's no one watching the delivery entrance below the Mexican restaurant. We can get her out that way."

Big Teeth still gripped the neckline of Sierra's blouse at the back. "And then what?" He shook Sierra.

"The Blue Devil van will be waiting for us. We can put her in it and take her to the boat at Homestead Marina."

"Why doesn't someone else take her?"

"Heathen wants us to see this thing to the end."

"I don't like this plan," said Big Teeth.

Ponytail stomped toward him. His face was only inches from the other man's. "You owe him big time. If you had been there at the boat for the distribution, Heathen never would have had to step in and be seen by her."

Big Teeth's shoulders slumped. "Give me a minute. I think I know how to get her out of here without being noticed."

"Thanks for being a team player," said Ponytail. Sarcasm and animosity tainted his words.

Big Teeth shoved Sierra toward the other man and left the room.

Ponytail reached out to catch her. "Whoa there, little lady."

She stepped away from him. She felt as though her mind and body were being squeezed from the outside like an anaconda suctioning around her, making it hard to breathe or think.

But she had to think…to come up with a plan. The window of the hotel room looked out on the marina. She ran toward it, surveying the ground below. Down there, a man dressed in casual clothes stalked the pier very deliberately. She recognized him as Mike Alvarez.

Please, look up here.

"Stand back from there." Ponytail lunged toward her and pulled her away from the window. He yanked the curtain shut.

Big Teeth entered the room. He wore a waiter's smock and pushed a room service cart. He lifted the skirt of the cart. "We can put her under here."

"She'll squawk."

Big Teeth grinned. "No, she won't." He pulled out his gun.

The last thing she remembered before her world went black was the gun hitting the back of her head.

SEVENTEEN

Joseph watched the monitors and paced. He squeezed one fisted hand with the other. There had to be something more he could do to find Sierra.

Baseball Hat man had offered him no other information. He'd been taken into custody by the rookie agent. The DEA would continue to question him. They might get more answers, but he had a feeling that would come too late for Sierra.

He stepped closer to the monitors. They couldn't cover everything. There had to be something they were missing.

Cindy stepped through the door. "Thought you could use an extra set of eyes."

"Thanks. I'm going down the hall to get a soda. You want anything?"

Cindy sat down in a chair and looked at the monitors. "I'm fine."

Joseph stepped out into the hallway. The

vending machine on the seventh floor had only sugary drinks. He headed down the stairs to the sixth floor to see if they had a better selection. When he stepped into the hallway, he saw a man with a long ponytail headed toward the elevator. A moment later, a room service attendant pushed a cart out of one of the rooms.

Joseph headed in the opposite direction, toward the vending machine. He glanced over his shoulder just as the room service attendant pushed the cart into the elevator. Sensing that he was being watched, the man looked in Joseph's direction and grinned.

Joseph's heart fluttered.

Something is not right with this picture.

The room service smock the man wore was clearly too small for him. And the man looked familiar.

He ran toward the elevator, but it was too late. He sprinted to the stairwell and pulled out his phone, then dialed Cindy's number. "Do you have a man watching the elevator?"

"Yes, on the ground floor. Where are you? You sound like you're running."

"Let me know if a man with a ponytail and a man pushing a room service cart get out." He bolted down several more flights of stairs.

His phone rang. "Yes." He had the sensation of a clock ticking inside his head.

"This is Agent Brewer. No one matching your description got out on the ground floor."

His heart sank. They could have gotten out on another floor, but the ground floor was the only one that would provide them with a route to escape.

He hung up and ran the remainder of the way to the ground floor. Bursting through the stairwell door, he searched the area, which was teeming with people. It would be easy enough to slip into the crowd. But the agent said no one matching his description had gotten out of the elevator.

He clicked Cindy's number. "Can you pull up the map of the building? Tell me if there is a service elevator they could have gotten onto on a different floor."

"Joseph, where are you?"

"Never mind, just tell me if there's a service elevator they could have gotten onto."

He heard the faint sound of computer keys clicking. "Yes, looks like it goes all the way down to the basement."

"Where is it located?" He turned side to side still watching the crowd. Several people bumped against him.

"Northeast end of the building, next to the Mexican restaurant," said Cindy. "Don't you have orders to do a desk job because of your injury?"

"My orders were to keep Sierra safe, and that's what I'm doing. Stay on the line. I need you to look at the map." He pushed through the crowd until he hurried down a side corridor. He spotted the elevator and dashed toward it. It looked like it didn't require a special key or code that only employees would have. The corridor was dark and only busy toward the upper end of it, where the Mexican eatery was.

"What do you need to know?"

DEA didn't have endless manpower. There had to be an exit they couldn't cover. He stepped into the elevator and pushed the button marked 0.

"Is there an exit out of the basement? One we didn't cover?" He pressed the phone against his ear as the doors of the elevator closed. The elevator jolted into motion as it carried him down one floor.

Cindy came back online. "There's a loading dock. The drone has been by there several times. No suspicious activity."

"This is just a hunch. But send the drone by there again. Let me know if you spot anything." He clicked off just as the elevator doors slid open.

The sound of women chattering and laughing reached his ears when he stepped out. He hurried down the hall and stood outside the door where the voices were coming from. The conversation was about children and shopping. He heard machines running. A laundry room? He stuck his head in the room. It was humid. White items whirred around in the dryers while two women stood at a table, folding napkins. A third woman stuffed towels into a washing machine.

The women stopped chatting and looked up at him.

"Are you lost?"

"Did two men come by here? Or maybe just one pushing a room service cart?"

One of the women at the table put her hand on her ample hip. "Oh, honey, those carts go directly back to a storage area on the main drag, where most of the restaurants are."

"Did you see a man with a ponytail come through here? Did anyone come through here?"

All the women shook their heads in unison.

"We've been pretty busy," said the woman loading towels.

"Thanks anyway." He was wasting valuable time. He hurried through the dark corridor, finding only storage rooms and wood pallets and piles of cardboard boxes. His spirits sank. Had he wasted valuable time on a wild goose chase?

His phone rang. It was Cindy.

"Yes?" His heartbeat drummed in his ears.

"Drone picked up something a little weird in the alley outside the loading dock."

"What is it?"

"A room service cart."

"Thanks, Cindy. I'm pretty sure that was where Sierra was. Can I get some extra manpower?"

"I'll let Alvarez know, but he probably won't want to call men off their posts until we've spotted Sierra for sure. Can't risk them getting out after we've pulled men off the exits."

"Got it. Understood." His heart revved into overdrive as he ran down the maze of hallways that must lead to the loading dock. The loading dock had a ramp to street level. He burst through the door beside the garage-sized door. Right away, he saw the abandoned room service cart. The driveway where freight was unloaded slanted downward and was wide enough for a truck to back up to. The alley itself was at ground floor level.

He hurried up the alley and out onto the street. The man with the ponytail had just closed the back of a van that advertised Blue Devil boat cleaning products. Joseph crouched behind a Dumpster and watched as the man with the ponytail got into the passenger seat and the van pulled away from the curb.

Joseph rushed up the street to where a man had just gotten off a motorcycle.

He flashed his badge. "I need your bike."

The man threw up his arms and stepped back. "Take it. Just get it back to me in one piece." He handed Joseph his helmet.

Joseph jumped on and turned the key in the ignition. He zoomed out into the street. Traffic was heavy. He spotted the van several vehicles ahead of him. He was grateful that the helmet hid his face as he wove through traffic to stay with the van.

The van navigated through several stoplights. Joseph pulled up beside the driver's side. The driver was a man he'd seen before, the muscular man with big teeth. The visor on the helmet hid Joseph's face from view.

There was no time to stop and alert the rest of the team that he was on to something. He didn't want to risk losing the van.

The blinker on the van clicked on as it took an exit ramp that led to the highway. Joseph leaned into the curve and followed the van. They traveled in moderate traffic. He was able to keep several cars between himself and the van but still tail it with ease.

After ten miles, the van turned onto a small two-lane road. Only one other car besides his motorcycle and the van traveled down the road.

He kept the car between himself and the van so he wouldn't be spotted. The signs they passed indicated they were headed toward a private marina called Homestead.

Before he got to the marina, Joseph pulled his borrowed motorcycle onto a shoulder of the road. He tore his helmet off and placed it on the seat of the bike. He could see the piers to the marina that stretched out into the water.

The parking lot beside the marina was gravel. The van came to a stop. Joseph hurried through the trees to get close to where the van was parked. Then the other car came to a stop, several parking spots away from the van.

A man and a woman holding a child who was maybe three or four got out of the car. The man ran ahead to untie their boat. There were five boats and two empty docking spaces. Besides the car and the van, there was only one other vehicle parked in the lot.

No one got out of the van.

Just more confirmation that the two men had Sierra and didn't want any witnesses.

He stepped back into the trees and clicked in Cindy's number, knowing that he might not get another chance to advise the team of where he was. He spoke in hushed tones as he explained the situation to Cindy and gave his location. "I know I don't have visual confirmation that Sierra is in that van, but sometimes where a life is concerned, you have to go with your gut."

"I understand," Cindy said. "I'll let Alvarez know. It's his call as to how the operation goes down."

The line went dead.

The man boarded the boat and helped his wife and child get on. The mother settled into a back seat with the kid. Once behind the wheel, the man maneuvered the boat out of the dock, glancing several times up at the van. Even they were wondering why the two men hadn't gotten out.

Joseph worked his way through the trees, getting as close to the van as he dared. The only way to get closer would be to run across the lot and hide behind the other parked car. He stared at the back of the van.

The men seemed to be waiting until the boat with the family was out of view.

All his instincts told him Sierra was in there. How easy would it be to run over there, yank open the doors and get her out? But if the doors were locked, he'd be discovered, too. If she was unconscious or tied up, all of that would cost valuable time he didn't have.

He made the decision to run to the car close to the van. From this side of the car, he'd have a clean shot at one of the men. Maybe in the ensuing panic, he could disable the other man, as well, and then get Sierra out of that van.

If Sierra was conscious, they could slip through the trees and back up to the motorcycle before the men had recovered. That was a big if. The better plan seemed to be to get behind the wheel of that van, leaving the men without transportation.

The boat with the family grew smaller and smaller.

The driver's side door clicked open and the kidnapper got out. Though he could not see the other side of the van, he heard the passenger side door click open. He had to assume both men were armed. He was outnumbered and out-armed. The only thing in his favor was the element of surprise.

He looked in Joseph's direction. Joseph took aim just as Sierra's kidnapper reached for his gun. Joseph got off one round. Before he had time to assess if he had hit his target, he ran to the bumper of the car, where he was less exposed.

The ensuing silence was deafening. Joseph grew keenly aware of his heart beating, of his breathing, of his shoes making noise in the gravel as he tried to reposition himself to get a view of what was going on.

Through the back window and the windshield

of the car, he could see only the top part of the van. There was no visible activity. Maybe the kidnapper, the one who had been driving, was lying on the ground beside the van, or maybe he'd retreated into the van. Maybe Ponytail had sought shelter back in the van, as well.

They were at a standoff. Up the road, he heard another car headed toward the area.

Footsteps sounded on the gravel behind him seconds before he felt a blow to his head that made black dots form around the rims of his vision again. He registered that Ponytail had raised the butt of his gun and hit him—just before his world went black.

EIGHTEEN

From the back of the van, conscious but not entirely coherent, Sierra picked up on the level of panic between her two abductors.

The back of the van swung open and an unconscious Joseph was tossed in like a bag of potatoes. These guys sure liked knocking people out.

"I been hit. I been hit," the man with the big teeth wailed while Ponytail got behind the wheel of the van.

"There's another car coming into the lot," said Ponytail. "This place is Grand Central Station. I'm not waiting around for it to clear out."

"We can't," said Big Teeth. "I'm bleeding. I need medical attention."

Ponytail started the van and peeled out of the lot, spitting gravel on his way back up to the road. "Would you quit being such a little girl? It looks like a flesh wound."

"What are we going to do? Drive around all day with these two?" said Big Teeth.

"Get on the line with Heathen. He can set something up. He doesn't want their bodies to be found, and he doesn't want witnesses." Ponytail pounded his fist on the steering wheel.

"I say we off them right now and then deal with the bodies later."

Big Teeth's words sent chills through Sierra.

"Keep a cool head, will you? I'm not going back to prison," said Ponytail.

Sierra gazed at Joseph, his long hair flopped over his face. He was so still, he looked almost dead. Only the swelling and deflating of his chest told her he was just unconscious.

The motion of the van smoothed out as they turned off the two-lane onto the highway. There were no windows in the back of the van. The only way she could see would be to lift her head and try to peer out the front window.

The better idea seemed to be to lie still and not alert the two angry men to the fact that she'd regained consciousness.

She lay on her side with her cheek pressed against the dirty carpet of the van. Her wrists were bound together with a necktie. She watched Joseph, praying for signs that he would wake up.

Big Teeth talked on the phone in hushed tones, punctuated with the occasional groan of pain. Though she couldn't be certain, it sounded like they were going to go back to the private marina once it was dark.

The van rolled down the highway.

"Take the next exit. I know a guy who can fix me up with some pain pills. Get this bullet out of me. We got time."

In the silence, she could hear the turn signal clicking and then the van jostled from side to side, indicating they had left the smooth surface of the highway.

Joseph's eyes fluttered open. He smiled when he saw her. She lifted her head, indicating he needed to come closer.

The noise of the van rumbling over the gravel road would block out her voice if she whispered. Still lying down, he scooted toward her. She put her lips very close to his ear.

"I know who Heathen is."

Joseph nodded and gave her a thumbs-up.

The van came to a stop before she could say anything more.

Big Teeth pushed open the passenger side door. "Check on those two, will you."

Joseph lay on his side, faking unconsciousness. Sierra did the same.

The driver's side door opened and shut. Outside, feet crunched on gravel. Her eyes shot open. She hoped her expression conveyed to

Joseph that she was wondering what the plan was. Were they going to try to subdue Ponytail when he opened the back door?

Joseph shook his head and closed his eyes again.

The back door of the van swung open. Ponytail wiggled her foot. He must have done the same to Joseph before she heard the back doors of the van easing shut.

While Ponytail paced around outside, Joseph lifted his head to peer through the windshield. He hid himself behind the seat, barely peeking out, then dropped back down to the van floor.

Joseph leaned close to her and whispered in her ear. "Looks like we're at a veterinarian's place out in the country." He reached over and undid the necktie that bound her hands. "The keys are not in the ignition. Slip out the back. Hurry."

She scooted toward the door, pressed the handle and eased it open until she had a sliver of a view. No sign of Ponytail, though she had to assume he might patrol around the back of the van.

She eased open the door and dropped onto the ground. Joseph was right behind her. He shut the door.

She heard footsteps on gravel, and both of them scurried around to the side of the van and bolted toward the first sign of cover, an old truck. They both rested on their bellies underneath the truck. She could see Ponytail's feet as he circled around the van. Nothing in the pace of his footsteps suggested alarm.

The vet's place was a one-story log cabin with corrals off to the side that appeared to extend around to the back of the structure. Two horses were visible. Beside the old truck, there was a horse trailer.

Joseph leaned close to Sierra and whispered, "Our priority is to get the information you have to the DEA. They took my phone and my gun when they knocked me out." His hand touched the back of her shoulder. "We may not get out of this alive, Sierra."

Joseph watched Sierra's eyes go wide with fear.

He'd done the math. They were up against two armed men prone to violence and not opposed to murder. If the vet was in the habit of providing painkillers and pulling bullets out of criminals, he would probably take the side of the two men, or at least stand back and let them do their dirty business.

He stood to stare into the cab of the truck. No keys in there, either. Escape didn't seem like a possibility.

Ponytail came back around the van. Joseph ducked down.

He weighed their options. Before the two men took off, they'd check the back of the van again and know that he and Sierra had escaped.

How long did it take to get a bullet out?

The best option seemed to be to get to a phone. That way, the DEA would know who Heathen was, and then he and Sierra could seek an escape. He didn't want the valuable information Sierra had to die with them. His work had to mean something, even if he didn't make it out of here.

The property was surrounded by trees. The log cabin had a big front window with a high counter. There had to be a phone there. He signaled for Sierra to head toward the trees. They'd have to find a back door. Ponytail would spot them if they went through the front.

They hurried through the trees and then slipped through the wooden fence, where a cow was kept. Still crouching low, they made their way toward the back door. Joseph eased it open. To one side were cages that contained a couple of cats and a small sleeping dog. On the other side was an exam room where the veterinarian, a hunched-over older man, stood dressing the shoulder of Big Teeth, who had taken his shirt off. The front desk lay straight ahead.

From the front of the office, Ponytail burst into the cabin. "They've escaped."

Both the vet and Big Teeth hurried into the reception area and then out to where the van was. Now was their chance. They dashed into the reception area and slipped behind the counter. He peered up. A cell phone sat on the higher part of the counter and a landline was on the lower part, where the computer was.

One of the men came back into the reception area and ran through to the back of the building.

"They couldn't have gotten far."

Sierra slipped underneath the desk where the computer was. Joseph pressed in beside her. The door slammed. They could hear the muffled sounds of the men as they shouted outside, coming up with a search plan. Joseph leaped up and grabbed the cell phone.

As they made their way toward the back door, he spotted a side door. The men would be circling the building, checking all the doors. Maybe one of them would head toward the trees to search there. He pulled Sierra toward the side door. They ran past what must be a supply room, filled with medical equipment and pet food. He eased open the side door and peered outside, and was greeted by a barrage of dogs barking. The large dogs were kept outside in kennels, and now they were alerting the pursuers to their whereabouts. Joseph shut the door. The dogs continued to bark.

They hurried back into the storage room. And then into the area that led to the back door. The side door opened and he heard footsteps coming toward them.

He pulled Sierra back toward a coatrack beside the cat cages. Sierra was behind a pair of coveralls that reached almost to the floor, and he sought concealment behind a longer coat. The coatrack was in the shadows, but if someone looked closely, they'd see their feet. Joseph turned his head sideways.

Someone marched through the area, his boots tapping the concrete floor, and swung open the back door. The dogs outside settled down and stopped barking. Only the faint sound of one man yelling orders at another reached his ears. At one point, he thought he heard a vehicle start up.

He turned his head the other way to a view of a tabby cat tilting her head and watching him before she lifted her front paw and started to clean it. The cat's back leg was bandaged, making balance a little tricky.

He waited for several more minutes before slipping out from behind the coat. He took Sierra's hand and once again pushed open the back door a sliver. The veterinarian holding a rifle was watching the trees and then looking back at the cabin.

He waited until the vet's back was to them before hurrying outside and crouching behind a chicken coop. Sierra slid in beside him. He could see the vet through the mesh of the chicken coop that contained only two chickens, which seemed undisturbed by their presence.

Sierra gripped his arm and whispered, "The horses."

Was she thinking they might escape on the horses? One of them had a bandaged leg, but the other one might be viable. It had a bridle, but no saddle. The horse that appeared not to have any serious injury was tethered to a fence post.

The veterinarian wandered a little deeper into the trees.

Now was their chance. They sprinted toward the horse that was tied up. While he freed the horse, Sierra opened the corral.

The vet emerged through the trees and shouted over his shoulder as he hurried toward them. Joseph got up on the horse. He reached a hand down so Sierra could swing a leg over the horse using his foot as a stirrup. She wrapped her arms around his waist and held on.

The old man rested his rifle on the fence and took aim just as Joseph spurred the horse into a gallop. He heard shouting behind him and a single rifle shot that went wild before they entered the shelter of the trees. The forest was thick enough that he slowed the horse to a trot.

They were going where no car could follow them. They came out into an open field filled with sheep. Joseph skirted around the edges of the herd. He had no idea where they were or how to get back to civilization. The phone he'd taken from the vet's office pressed against his chest pocket. All they needed was five minutes to make the call. At least then they could get Sierra's information to the DEA, even if they couldn't pinpoint where they were.

The name of the veterinarian clinic had been on a sign on the front door. He'd glanced at it, reading it backward. With his energy focused on escape, he didn't have time to jog his memory.

He heard the sound of a dirt bike behind him. Of course, the vet had a motorcycle. And it looked like Ponytail was going to run them down with it.

He spurred the horse into a gallop and headed back toward the trees, hoping to find some terrain that would be too rough for even a motorcycle to follow. Instead the trees opened up to a dirt road. Up ahead, the van was coming toward them just as the sputter and hum of the dirt bike grew menacingly close.

They were trapped.

NINETEEN

The sound of the motorcycle grew louder, and the van hurtled toward them. One of the men must have jumped in the van, patrolling the road, and was headed back toward the vet's place. Agitated, the horse took several steps backward and jerked its head up and down.

"Giddyap." Joseph lifted the reins and directed the horse off the side of the road. The horse plunged into the ditch next to the gravel road. He steered the horse perpendicular to the road across an open field.

Shots fired behind them. Heart racing, Sierra held on tighter and glanced over her shoulder. Whoever was in the van had fired shots from the driver's side. The hum of the motorcycle remained close at their heels.

The motorcycle with Ponytail on it came up beside them. The horse stepped sideways and then reared up. Ponytail continued to rev the motorcycle, doing circles around the horse.

The horse dropped back down on all fours, but remained agitated and hard to control.

Joseph waited for an opening, spurred the horse and bolted for another cluster of trees. The motorcycle nipped at their heels until they got into the trees and were able to weave through the aspens.

The sound of the motorcycle grew fainter. The engine sputtered and revved, died out and came back to life. Ponytail was having a hard time navigating the tight terrain.

The trees grew so close together, the horse finally balked at passing through them. Sierra slipped off the horse and Joseph followed. Still keeping a solid pace, he led the horse through the aspen grove. From time to time, the faint, faraway sound of the motorcycle fell on her ears.

Joseph pulled the phone out of his breast pocket. "Call Cindy." He recited the number for her. "Tell her what you know."

Both of them continued to walk at a brisk pace while she pressed the numbers. Cindy picked up right away. "Cindy, this is Sierra. I don't have much time."

"Where are you? Is Joseph with you?"

"Yes. Listen, you need to look into who is behind Blue Devil boat cleaning products. I think the man I saw in the forest is connected to that business. Also, the dispatcher for the city cops is feeding him info."

"Got it. Are you safe? Can we come for you?"

Sierra looked over at Joseph. "I don't know where we are."

The trees had cleared, and they were out in the open again.

"Hurry," said Joseph.

He must have seen or heard something that had alarmed him. She didn't notice anything, but she would trust his eyes and ears any day. "We were at a private marina," he said. "Homestead Marina."

"Yes," said Sierra. She spoke to Cindy. "We were at a private marina outside Scenic View, Homestead Marina, and then we were on the highway for about twenty minutes and we came to a veterinarian's place."

The name came back to him. "Creekside Medical," said Joseph. He glanced around nervously and then mounted the horse.

"Creekside Medical," she repeated into the phone, amazed at Joseph's powers of observation.

Then she heard what had put Joseph on high alert. Though she could not tell which direction the motorcycle was coming from, the mechanical clang of the engine grew louder and more intense.

She clicked off the phone and handed it back to Joseph to put in his pocket before getting back on the horse.

The horse took off at a gallop through the open field. The motorcycle had circled around the trees and was making a beeline for them. Sierra wrapped her arms around Joseph and pressed close to him. Even as her heart pounded and fear invaded every thought, she felt safe with Joseph, knowing that he would do everything in his power to keep both of them alive.

The motorcycle hounded them for at least twenty minutes and then the roar of the engine stopped. Joseph kept his eye straight ahead as the horse slowed when the terrain shifted from flat ground to low hills.

Sierra spoke to him over his shoulder. "I think he ran out of gas. He stopped and he's opening the tank."

The horse was tiring, slowing down into a canter. "This horse can't go much farther without rest."

They were not by any means safe yet. Would the DEA be able to find them with the information they had been able to supply? How long would those men continue to search for them?

He heard the bubbling of a creek.

"Let's give this horse a rest, see if we can

contact Cindy and give her some more information about our location."

Sierra slipped off the horse and he followed. He pulled the horse toward the sound of the running water, where he lowered his head and drank. He leaned over and stroked the horse's neck. "This old fella did good, but I really don't think we can run him any more."

Sierra came to stand beside him. When the horse raised his head, she combed through his mane. "Plus, he was at a vet's. No signs that he had an external injury, but maybe he was on the mend from some kind of sickness."

He liked that she stood beside him, their shoulders touching, the evening sun shining on them. He wished that they could stay frozen in the softness of the moment. Though they'd been given a brief reprieve, danger lurked just outside the perimeter of their quiet moment. Those men were not going to give up easily.

They weren't going to get any farther on the horse, and really, the closer they could stay to the vet's place without being caught by the three men, the better chance they had of the DEA being able to pinpoint their location.

The terrain had grown rougher, more mountainous.

He took out the phone and stared at it. There wasn't much battery left on it. "Do you recognize any of the larger landmarks around here, a mountain peak or anything?"

Sierra shook her head.

"I say we leave the horse here. He'll find his way back to the vet's." He pointed toward a hillside. "We get to a high spot, alert the DEA of our location and wait it out. If those men do come after us, we'll be able to see them coming."

She nodded.

He slapped the horse on its haunches and it took off running, back in the general direction of the veterinarian's.

Joseph shook his head. "They always go back to where the food is."

They took off hiking up the mountain to a spot that provided them with a clear view of the valley below. Joseph stood up and studied the landscape. The metal roof of the vet's place glistened in the sun. He saw no signs of any of the three men. He spoke to Cindy on the phone for only a few minutes, alerting her of their approximate location.

Then he hunkered down beside Sierra, who was hidden behind some thick brush. They waited for at least forty-five minutes. From time to time, he lifted his head above the brush to see if their pursuers were coming for them. At one point, he saw the van moving up the road in the distance, but no one came near the high point where they were hiding.

It was a reprieve to sit next to Sierra in silence, surrounded by the beauty of nature. In their run from the pursuers, Sierra's long dark hair had worked free of the ponytail she kept it in. She smiled at him, her blue eyes dancing, and then she tilted her head toward the sky and closed her eyes. "The setting sun feels good."

"Yes, it's nice." Even though they weren't safe yet, it was wonderful to be here with her, enjoying how beautiful she looked. He liked the way she leaned close to him. He knew the moment was only temporary, but he relished it all the same. He wanted to tell her he loved her even if she rejected him after the way he'd been so closed off to her. She mattered more to him than his job.

Before he could find the courage to speak, the distant whir of a helicopter interrupted his thoughts.

"They found us." Sierra's words held joy.

She stood up and waved, and the helicopter drew near.

"Let's get down to a flatter area so they can pick us up," said Joseph.

They hurried down toward the grassy valley as the helicopter hovered and then descended.

His elation, though, was short-lived. The

doors of the helicopter opened and a man aimed a rifle in their direction. Seconds before he fell himself, Joseph watched as Sierra's rag doll body crumpled to the ground.

TWENTY

Sierra awoke to the rhythm of waves beating against a boat. Her head felt like it was stuffed full of rocks. Her body was stiff. Joseph lay beside her on his stomach, his face turned to one side away from her.

She touched his back, feeling him inhale and exhale shallowly.

They were in the hull of some kind of fairly large boat. The labels on the boxes indicated that food was stored here. Footsteps pounded above her.

She rose on wobbly feet and walked over to a ladder with a trapdoor at the top. She climbed the ladder and pushed on the trapdoor. Either it was latched on the outside, or someone had placed a weight on it.

Joseph started to stir.

She hurried over to him as he sat up, holding his head. "They must have used some sort of tranquilizer on us." Joseph rubbed the sore spot on his good shoulder where the dart had sunk in.

She slumped down beside him and tilted her head toward where the footsteps were pounding. "Do you suppose the DEA was able to get there in time and track us?"

He touched his pocket. "The phone is gone."

"Probably won't work out here anyway." Her throat went tight with fear. "I bet they're going through with the plan to dump us in some remote part of the lake."

He reached over and wrapped an arm around her, drawing her close.

"They'll probably kill us and then weight the bodies so we won't ever be found." A shiver ran down her spine as she spoke.

Joseph squeezed her upper arm. He turned toward her, touched her chin and guided her head so she was looking at him. She took in those big brown eyes, the soft wavy hair and that always-gentle expression that made her think he looked more like a kind friend than a DEA agent.

He leaned close to her, resting his palm on her cheek. His lips brushed over hers. The warmth, the electrical stir of energy flooded through every muscle and covered her skin. He pressed his mouth on hers and deepened the kiss.

He drew back, brushing her hair behind her

ear and gazing at her. His light touch on her ear sent a surge of heat straight to her heart.

"I wanted to give you a real kiss."

"I thought the first kiss was real. It was for me, anyway," she said.

Even in the dim light, she watched his eyes brighten and spark to life. "It was for me, too." He kissed her again. "I just wanted to make sure there was no confusion."

Death was just around the corner for both of them. She saw no way to escape, and Joseph probably didn't, either. She wanted to stay in this moment forever, basking in the warmth of his affection.

They heard the sound of footsteps and the trapdoor creaking open.

Joseph kissed her one more time. "I wish all of this could have ended differently."

Feet appeared on the ladder. Once he was down the ladder, Ponytail, with a gun in a holster at his side, stood with his arms crossed, glaring at them.

Another man came down the ladder and stepped toward them. She knew that face. The image on the monitor was burned into her mind now. The man they called Heathen stalked toward them.

"Well, it seems you two have had quite the

wild ride." His smiled, but his eyes remained dull and dark.

If this man—the one they had been after all along—was showing himself, it meant for sure they were going to die.

Heathen paced back and forth. He held a pair of leather gloves that he slapped against his palm as he spoke. "I have to give you credit. The DEA works fast. They were hacking into the computers of Blue Devil cleaning products probably only minutes after you gave them the information. They even managed to pick up my girlfriend. It was convenient to have the dispatcher for the city police on my side. Cops talk within hearing distance of her, cops' wives confided in her and of course all emergency calls came through her. More than once, she was able to delay getting the cops dispatched so my men could get out of harm's way."

Sierra's heartbeat drummed in her ears. She felt herself going numb even as the memory of Joseph's kiss played around the corners of her mind. She reached for Joseph's hand, lacing her fingers with his, grateful that her final memory would be realizing that Joseph cared about her in the same way she cared about him.

Heathen stalked toward them. He kneeled and turned her face so she was forced to look at him.

Joseph jerked in reaction to Heathen touching her.

Heathen did not take his eyes off Sierra as he spoke, punctuating each word. "Don't. You. Dare. Try. Anything."

Joseph squeezed her hand tighter.

Heathen burst to his feet. "The DEA can't outsmart me. I have more resources than you could possibly imagine." He slapped the gloves together one more time and stalked toward the ladder before turning back to face them. "Don't worry. This will all be over in a little while." His voice dripped with sarcasm. "This time it will be done right. I'm here to make sure of that."

Sierra felt her blood run cold when Heathen winked at them. Heathen headed up the ladder. Ponytail followed behind them.

Silence like a shroud fell around them. She closed her eyes and focused on the sound of the boat engine.

Joseph pushed himself to his feet. "We're not tied up. There has to be some way we can get out of here."

"The reason they didn't tie us up is because they know we can't escape." She could feel herself shutting down, giving up.

Joseph paced around the room, moving boxes, examining the walls of the boat. "There has to be something we can work with here." He stopped and stared at the ceiling as though an idea had occurred to him. He reached his hands out to her and pulled her to her feet. He wrapped his arms around her and closed his eyes. "Oh, God, we need Your help. Please."

His prayer sent a spark of life through her. He held her close for a moment longer.

The trapdoor opened, and Ponytail came in with another man who held a gun on them.

Ponytail pushed her toward the ladder. "Watch your step, pretty lady."

Once they were on deck, a pillowcase was slipped over her head. Someone grabbed her hands and wrapped restraints around her wrists.

She'd caught only a glimpse of the landscape around her. They were in a sort of cove. The seaplane that had probably carried the assassins earlier rested on the water off to one side.

She heard Ponytail's voice. "Okay, kid, earn your stripes." Footsteps pounded across the deck.

Joseph stood close enough to her that his arm brushed against hers. She sensed that someone else was close, as well—the kid who needed to earn his stripes, whoever that was.

Her heart pounded wildly, and she had the sensation of an elephant sitting on her chest.

Let's just get it over with. Joseph and I will be with God in the twinkling of an eye.

The DEA had the information they needed. For all his arrogance, she was certain Heathen would be taken down eventually. The boat continued to sway as the waves lapped against it.

What was the delay? Did the kid delight in tormenting them? A single footstep very close to her sounded on the floorboards.

A hand reached up toward her neck.

She jerked back.

"It's all right," said a voice. The hand touched the pillowcase and removed it.

In the dimness of evening, she recognized the man in front of her. Clive, the addict who had been on the boat previously because he owed a debt to the dealers.

He held up a hypodermic needle. "I'm supposed to knock you out with this and throw you in, attached to the weights." He reached over and untied Sierra's wrists. "You're a good person. You tried to help me. I can at least do something right in my life and let you go. Heathen will be listening for the sound of two bodies falling into the water. Take the weights and jump in."

Once she was untied, Sierra turned toward Joseph, pulled his hood off and untied him.

"Hurry," said Clive. "Don't jump at the same time. He'll be listening for two splashes with a pause in between."

"Thank you, Clive. You've done the right thing." Sierra looked at Joseph.

"You go first." She picked up the weight, which was a brick with holes and a rope attached. Sierra stared down at the dark water for only a moment before plunging in. The weight pulled her deep into the water. She let go of it and bobbed close to the surface. She remained underwater, making her way toward the shore.

She heard a splash behind her. She swam a little farther, trying not to make a sound. A moment later, Joseph grabbed her ankle. She righted herself and treaded water.

Joseph bobbed in the water, as well. "My guess is Heathen is taking off in that plane. I say we hijack him."

Before she could respond, voices from the boat grew louder. Men had come out on deck. Sierra and Joseph slipped beneath the surface of the water and continued to swim. She poked her head up at eye level to get her bearings. The men were no longer on the deck of the boat.

Joseph was just a few feet ahead of her, moving through the water like a trout as he made his way toward the seaplane. When they were within feet of the plane, the sound of a motorboat reached her ears. Heathen must be coming this way.

Joseph swam around to the far side of the

plane so they wouldn't be spotted. "There's probably a pilot in there waiting. We'll have to take him out." He pulled himself up on one float of the plane. "Hurry, we don't have much time."

He climbed in and reached down to help her. "No pilot?"

"Heathen must be flying the plane himself." He pulled her up. "Or his pilot is coming with him in that boat."

Her belly rested on the floor of the plane while Joseph hurried around to the front. Crouching low, he peered through the front window.

"He's on his way. It looks like there are three guys in the boat."

Fear seized her mind. How could they overtake three men and hope to stay alive?

TWENTY-ONE

As he led Sierra around to the third section of seats, Joseph assessed what he had to work with. Chances were, Heathen kept at least one gun for protection somewhere on the plane. Sure enough, he spotted a handgun next to the copilot's seat, rushed over and grabbed it.

"Slip down there in the shadows." He pointed toward the far side of the plane.

Sierra disappeared from view as she crouched behind a seat that faced the open door.

The boat was coming around to the side so Heathen could board.

Joseph grabbed a raincoat that was flung over the back of a seat. He squeezed in beside Sierra, using the coat to conceal himself.

He felt the plane rocking and heard footsteps. He couldn't tell how many men had gotten on board. He also heard voices, so at least two men were on the plane. Then he heard the sound of the boat head back toward the larger boat. Maybe only two men had gotten on board.

The plane's engine whirred and sputtered. The plane jerked forward and then lifted off. Joseph eased the coat away from his face and lifted his head. Heathen was flying the plane and Ponytail, who must function as his body-guard, sat in the copilot's seat.

The men had no reason to be on their guard. As far as they knew, he and Sierra were at the bottom of the lake.

The conversation between the two men was about Heathen having to hide out before trying to leave the country because the DEA would be watching all possible escape routes.

Joseph didn't want to risk crashing. It sounded like they were going to land somewhere close until Heathen could escape. The safe thing for Joseph to do was wait it out. Once the plane landed, he could catch the two men by surprise, restrain them and then get in touch with the DEA.

He slipped back beneath the coat. Sierra was close enough to him to rest her hand on his fore-arm. It felt like a way of saying that she was here with him.

Both of them were soaking wet from their es-cape. The flight seemed to take forever. After what felt like most of the night, the plane began its descent. It touched down several times, skimming the water and then coming to a stop.

Joseph leaped to his feet, knowing that Heathen would be preoccupied with shutting down the plane. Ponytail must have sensed his presence, because he turned slightly. Joseph aimed to disable, not kill Ponytail. The shot nicked Ponytail's upper arm, causing him to double over.

Heathen had time to grab a gun that must have been stored in the cockpit. He aimed at Joseph, who dove behind the seat for cover. Heathen pushed open the pilot's door and splashed down into the water.

Joseph peered out the window. They were at a private residence. The large house was completely dark. He didn't see any other houses close by.

Sierra burst up and headed toward the side door, while Ponytail was still doubled over and in pain. Joseph was right behind her.

She pushed open the door and then released the dinghy that inflated by pulling a cord. Both of them grabbed paddles and hurried around the plane.

Heathen's head bobbed up and down in the water. Joseph waited until Heathen pulled himself up on the pier. They couldn't let him get to the house. There was no telling what kind of firearms he had in there, or extra muscle.

"Stop rowing." The boat bobbed in the water. His gun wavered up and down. He squeezed off two rounds. Heathen kept running toward the house. At first, Joseph thought he had missed his mark, but then he noticed Heathen favoring one of his legs.

The boat came to shore just as Heathen threw open the door and disappeared inside.

Ponytail probably wouldn't be able to swim very fast with his injury. Maybe not at all.

He only hoped there were no other thugs waiting inside to ambush them. The boat drew near to the shore. They jumped out and ran the remaining distance to the house.

"You stay out here. It's safer," Joseph said, then hurried around to the side of the house, searching for another point of entry. The house remained dark.

He found an unlocked side door and entered, ready to shoot. He pressed his back against a wall. As near as he could tell, he was in some sort of storage area filled with cubbies and places to hang coats. There was nothing stored in the cubbies, and no coats hung on the racks.

He entered a living room, where two suitcases sat by the door. Judging from the lack of personal items, this was probably a vacation rental. Joseph leaned against a wall and listened in the dark.

He worked his way down the hall and into the kitchen. The lights burst on. Heathen rose up from behind the counter and tossed a knife at Joseph. The blade grazed his cheek and the cut skin stung.

The room went dark again.

He heard tapping sounds. Someone moving around the room in the dark?

"Might as well give up now, Heathen. I've got a gun on you." He reached his free hand out toward the wall, trying to find the light switch.

He heard more noise. Pots banging against each other and then a dull thud. He felt along the wall with his free hand for the light switch. He winced from the pain in his own shoulder and his bloody cheek.

The lights came on, and Sierra popped up from behind the counter holding a cast-iron frying pan. "I know you said to wait outside, but that's just not my style."

He hurried around to her side of the counter where Heathen lay on his stomach, out cold. His lower leg was soaked in blood from where Joseph had shot him. "About time one of those guys got knocked unconscious instead of us," he said as he gathered Sierra into his arms.

Within twenty minutes, the DEA arrived at the vacation rental and took both men into custody. Joseph watched as Heathen was hauled away to a DEA vehicle.

Cindy came and stood beside Joseph. "His real name is Roy Basker. Blue Devil cleaning products is a legit business. They do a lot of international business and attend boat shows around the world."

"So plenty of chances for smuggling drugs," Joseph said.

"We are pretty sure he's the main distributor for the Northwest. Sierra's ID will go a long way toward putting him away for good," said Cindy.

Joseph shifted his weight and glanced over at Sierra who sat on the porch swing. His heart leapt at the sight of her. She looked beautiful and forlorn at the same time.

Cindy said, "We picked up a bunch of the secondary players at the hotel, as well. You and Sierra can help us ID even more. Gonna be a lot fewer drugs flowing through this area thanks to you two."

"Yes, we both deserve credit." He kept his eyes on Sierra. "Would you excuse me for a minute?" He walked over and sat down beside her.

Sierra stared out at the water while the agents bustled around the house and seaplane, collecting evidence.

Sierra turned to look in his eyes. "Don't you want to be out there where all the action is?"

He wrapped his arm around her. "I'm right where I want to be."

"For now?"

He sensed despair or sadness behind her words. He looked into her blue eyes, touching her chin. "No, forever. I meant what I said when I kissed you the second time. It wasn't just because I thought we were going to die."

Light came into her eyes, and her lips parted.

He leaned in and kissed her, and then rested his forehead against hers. "Here's to countless real kisses and a lifetime together."

She touched his cheek, her eyes searching. "Really? No more pretend?"

"It was never pretend for me," he said.

She kissed him lightly. "Me, either."

"Marry me, Sierra. I don't know what it will look like, but let's build a life together."

Her whole face glowed. "You mean you want to stay here in Scenic View? What will you do?"

Joseph shrugged. "I don't know. I hear the skateboard shop needs a manager. I just know this war can be fought on different fronts. I want to help you with the kids." He turned to face her, taking both her hands in his. "More than anything I want to spend my life with you. What do you say?"

She squeezed his hands and smiled. "Yes, Joseph, I will marry you."

With that, he took her in his arms and held his future wife, wanting only to stay in that moment and never let go of the woman he loved.

* * * * *

*If you enjoyed this story,
look for these other stories
by Sharon Dunn:*

Hidden Away
Thanksgiving Protector
Big Sky Showdown

Dear Reader,

I hope you enjoyed the wild adventure Sierra and Joseph went on and watching them fall in love. Because of choices she made as a teenager and her broken family life, Sierra carries a lot of shame about her past. Hers is far from the perfect family. Yet she chooses to love her father despite the pain he brought into her life, and she works at forgiveness toward her stepmother.

It would be easy for Sierra to think she can't do anything for God because of her past, yet instead she chooses to pay it forward and love kids whom others have given up on. I can't tell you how many times I have said or done something that made me feel like I was not worthy of God's love and certainly couldn't do anything to make a difference for Him.

It's easy to stay in that defeated place, but it's not where God wants us to be. He never expected us to be perfect. That's why there is opportunity for repentance and starting over each day. His mercies are new every morning. He loves us and wants the best for us. I am so grateful we serve such a loving God.

Blessings,

Sharon Dunn

Get 4 FREE REWARDS!

We'll send you 2 FREE Books plus 2 FREE Mystery Gifts.

Harlequin® Heartwarming™ Larger-Print books feature traditional values of home, family, community and most of all—love.

FREE Value Over **$20**

YES! Please send me 2 FREE Harlequin® Heartwarming™ Larger-Print novels and my 2 FREE mystery gifts (gifts worth about $10 retail). After receiving them, if I don't wish to receive any more books, I can return the shipping statement marked "cancel." If I don't cancel, I will receive 4 brand-new larger-print novels every month and be billed just $5.49 per book in the U.S. or $6.24 per book in Canada. That's a savings of at least 19% off the cover price. It's quite a bargain! Shipping and handling is just 50¢ per book in the U.S. and 75¢ per book in Canada*. I understand that accepting the 2 free books and gifts places me under no obligation to buy anything. I can always return a shipment and cancel at any time. The free books and gifts are mine to keep no matter what I decide.

161/361 IDN GMY3

Name (please print)

Address   Apt. #

City   State/Province   Zip/Postal Code

Mail to the **Reader Service:**
IN U.S.A.: P.O. Box 1341, Buffalo, NY 14240-8531
IN CANADA: P.O. Box 603, Fort Erie, Ontario L2A 5X3

Want to try two free books from another series? Call 1-800-873-8635 or visit www.ReaderService.com.

HOME on the RANCH